THE PASSIONATE SCRIBE

REKINDLING THE FIRE • BOOK THREE

MARCUS & MISTY OAKWOOD

THE PASSIONATE SCRIBE

Copyright © 2020 Marcus & Misty Oakwood

All rights reserved.

Published by Pax Ardsen

This is a work of fiction. Any similarity between the characters and situations within its pages and places or persons, living or dead, is unintentional and coincidental.

❀ Created with Vellum

CONTENTS

PROLOGUE: THE NEXT STEP

y toes curled into the soft green grass of the meadow. The next step took me past the edge of the woods and out from under the canopy. Clouds shaped like the animals that roamed wild through the forest decorated a brilliant blue sky. My gaze was pulled to the edge of the woods across the way, where the midnight black jaguar stood, watching me with hunger blazing in his eyes.

But the hunger wasn't to kill and consume me. No, his goal was something far more sensual.

The lithe feline stalked toward me, ensnaring me with its piercing stare. The magnetism of our connection lifted me off the ground, propelling me to him. I was powerless to stop myself from walking toward the danger, as if I didn't care, as if I didn't see his sharp teeth, his wicked claws, his unnaturally intelligent gaze holding me fast.

I knew this beast. He had been engaged to another of his kind... until he laid eyes on me. Love—no, destiny— surpassed all conventional wisdom and common sense, and we couldn't keep apart any longer. As I was pulled closer to him, each piece of my clothing fluttered away, and I was powerless. Yet, I didn't wish to stop—in fact, I yearned for the feel of his hard body against mine.

He began to shift, his strong feline shoulders rising up as his whole body launched itself onto its powerful hindquarters. Moving into a standing position, he turned his face to me as it rearranged from beautiful cat to stunningly masculine human, his naked skin almost as dark as his luscious jaguar fur. I floated to his grasp, nearly naked, and he reached for me. His green eyes had deepened, the color of longing intensifying with his humanity.

I couldn't entirely suppress my fear. Even though I wanted this, even though I begged for it, even though I died a million little deaths waiting for his touch.

"Take me, Jalen," I murmured, so close now that I felt heat rising off his ebony skin. His forelegs finished morphing into human arms, complete with rippling biceps, sinewy forearms, and powerful hands. I closed my eyes, awaiting the ecstasy of his touch.

The last piece of my clothing melted away, and I was completely bare, basking in his devouring stare. My heartbeat drove a rhythm in my chest, echoed by the visible pulsing in his unsheathed, uncut member, quivering inches from my aching sex, and I was desperate to engulf him completely.

He let out a feline growl as he lifted my left leg to my hip, then plunged his rod past my waiting lips, deep into my womanhood, slick with feminine dew. He wrapped his arms around me, his breath hot on my neck, his fingers running claw like through my hair. It was as if a bastion of magic burst forth within me. My pleasure built slowly, driving my breaths out in short gasps. His breathing, too, became labored.

"I don't understand the emotions you unearth in me," he murmured into my ear. "I am betraying my family, my loved ones—my prowl—for a human."

"I cannot resist you," I admitted through my gasps. "I'm powerless. As soon as you look into my eyes, I am yours."

"We are both slave to it," he growled, as he plundered my channel with his staff—deeper, faster, and harder. I grunted with each of his forceful thrusts. My walls were electrified. My skin tingled from his touch, and I cried out with need and desire. My sex had never been this filled before, never dripped with nectar for anyone.

"Oh, Jalen," I moaned, "don't stop! I need you deeper inside me. I've never felt this before."

"It's the magic of love between us," he whispered into my ear. "The werejaguars have always known it, but it's most intense when we bond to a human. It has nearly destroyed us in the past."

"And you're destroying my heart," I said.

THE WAY TO MY HEART

I stare at the screen and shake my head. "Blech. *Destroying my heart?*" I hit the delete key. "Come on, Rachel, get it together." The sex scene got me too turned on and distracted.

My phone buzzes. I glance at the clock in the corner of my monitor—1:30 a.m. I should have been asleep hours ago. Who's calling me this late?

Then I calculate the time difference. It's 10:30 a.m. in Zurich, where Jalen has been for the last two weeks. I look at the screen. Sure enough, it's him—my *husband* Jalen, not the sexy werejaguar of my story—wanting a video chat.

I rush into my bedroom with the phone, catching a quick look in the mirror above the dresser. My purple hair is a little flat, but my large brown eyes still have some sparkle left in them from the day. I have to keep reminding myself that Jalen likes the way I look—the round face I think is too circular, the button nose I think is too small, the white skin I think makes me look pallid. I sit on the bed, shake my hair from my face, and take a deep breath as I answer.

"Hey, you," I say.

His face appears on screen. Even after ten years of marriage, I'm still amazed that any man this good-looking is my husband. His eyes, a rich brown, are the first thing people notice because they are large, expressive, and mysterious. His jawline is strong but not sharp, and his kissable lips can both reveal a gorgeous smile or a troubled frown. He keeps his black hair cropped short, but it still provides contrast with his umber skin, smooth and blemish-free—not like the freckles that dot my nose and cheeks. Behind him, a bright yellow sign shines, showing a left arrow to Heathrow Express and a right arrow to the London Underground.

"Hey, beautiful," he says.

"Did your plane get delayed?"

"Not exactly."

My heart sinks. He was supposed to land at SFO in eight hours and be home in time to have lunch with me.

"Client emergency," he says. "I was supposed to change planes at Heathrow, but when I landed, I got a message from Roger that I need to go straight to Pointbridge Partners. They're talking about moving their investments to another firm."

It's an important meeting—Pointbridge is Jalen's biggest client—so I keep the disappointment off my face. "How much longer?"

"Two more days. Today I'll be at the Pointbridge site, and then Roger wants me to come to the office on Tuesday. They rebooked me on the direct to SFO Tuesday afternoon. I should be home by midnight."

"It's really not fair that they keep doing this to you. To *us*."

He sighs. "I know. It's only for a little while longer, though."

He said that six months ago. "It's just that it's kind of prime baby-making time. The window's open *now*."

"Oh. Shit." His face falls and eyes turn down. "Maybe I can get out of it and come home."

"I expected you home *tonight*. The timing would have been excellent."

"All right. Look, the client needs me today, and the flight to SFO is gone anyway. Maybe I can postpone my meeting with Roger and be home tomorrow."

"My tomorrow, or your tomorrow?"

He leans back in the seat. "Oh, crap. It must be late there. I didn't wake you up, did I?"

The hot werejaguar, named for my husband, forms in my mind, and has delicious, raw sex with my stand-in. "Nope. I was up late."

"Up late?"

"Working through a book." Is it a lie to imply that I'm reading a book, not writing one? I haven't told Jalen about the stories I write yet. They're really just to get me through the times he's not here, which lately are more and more frequent and last longer each trip.

"You're reading this late? Don't you have a presentation in the morning?"

I keep my tone playful. "You're the one who called *me*. And don't you have an unhappy client to see?"

"Yeah. I'm getting a cab as soon as I'm off this call."

"Too bad you're in the airport. We could do stuff."

His eyes sparkle. "If I can't change my flight, maybe we could video chat again tonight."

"You'll be up that late? I'll be off at five. That's midnight there, right?"

"One in the morning." He clears his throat. "Maybe *not* tonight. But I'll see you Wednesday evening."

"Yeah, okay."

"I love you."

"Love you too. Kick butt at the client's office."

We hang up. I should go to bed and get to sleep. 6:00 a.m. will come awfully early, and I need to be sharp for the presentation.

But I know if I don't get myself off, I'll be up even longer, like I was on Friday. I tossed and turned most of the night, the buzz between my legs refusing to go away.

I've been cheated. Two weeks without Jalen. Fourteen days without his soft lips on mine. Without his warm, slightly rough hands on my breasts. Without him sliding into bed beside me naked, his erection an exclamation point in the long sentence of the day.

I need him. I'm empty and there's an ache inside me tonight. The bed is cold on his side.

When we moved to Sacramento, he got a job with a boutique financial services company, and I accepted a position at a tech startup.

Two years later, I got laid off, but I found a less stressful job as a project manager at the State Infrastructure Board, and he took a better job at Woodward Reynolds. That's when he started traveling. A couple of trips a quarter became one trip a month, and then when the firm got purchased by a Swiss banking conglomerate, that once-a-month trip went from three days in New York to two weeks in Zurich.

Not that I envied him. Sure, *vacationing* in Europe would

be nice, but this was no boondoggle. The trip from Sacramento to Zurich required two plane changes, and he'd often be traveling for twenty-six or twenty-eight hours straight. Lately, he'd been driving the hundred miles to SFO, braving the horrific Bay Area traffic, and taking the eleven-hour direct flight.

We've been trying to start a family, but with him out of the country literally half the month, the timing hasn't been great. I promised myself I'd never have an ovulation calendar, but what do you know? Here I am, entering basal thermometer numbers into a spreadsheet. Never expected to be project managing getting knocked up.

It used to be, when we both got home from work, we couldn't keep our hands off each other. Now, when we both get home, he can barely keep his eyes open. He's often out of bed before I even get up. By the time his circadian rhythm gets back on track, when he starts going to bed at ten instead of six o'clock, and when I finally choose the evening I'll show off my new lingerie, he's leaving for Zurich again.

Lather, rinse, repeat.

For a year.

I'm not happy with this arrangement. Jalen keeps telling me it's temporary. "Just a little more time, babe," he'd say, kissing the side of my face. "The next step up the ladder will be the one that gets us where we need to be."

Does he think the grass will be greener when he gets the promotion? Because I'm not sure things will improve much. His boss doesn't travel any less than he does. She has three kids, and Jalen tells me she constantly complains about the ridiculous travel schedule the Zurich office insists upon.

Although I could barely get the stress of Jalen's job out of my mind these last few months, I've been just as horny as I was when we were in college. So, about half a year ago, I started taking matters into my own hands, as it were.

I read some smutty books.

There was one paranormal romance in particular that got me—a woman who fell in love with three werewolves who were all fighting for dominance in their pack. *The Alpha Wolfpack of Rivermoon* was the first book of its kind that I had ever read, and it made me, well, *feel* things. Things I hadn't felt in a long time.

It's not like it was *Moby Dick* or *Little Women*. It was barely even *Fifty Shades of Grey*. But boy, was it *hot*. I could feel the desire rising off the characters' bodies as they tangled. Three of the most spectacular men-beasts ever created were drooling over her body, and still the woman had a huge self-esteem problem and didn't think she was pretty.

Okay, so confession time: I feel like that. I feel like that a *lot*.

See, Jalen was *the* guy at Montrose High School, just outside of Phoenix. He was a three-sport athlete, plus he was a great student. On top of that, he was the best-looking guy in school. Tall and muscular, with deep brown eyes that made people stare. People were drawn to him. When he opened his mouth, his smooth baritone, eloquence, and heartfelt tone made people listen. He was the class homecoming king the first three years.

So when he asked me out during our senior year, I wondered if it was a prank.

I wasn't a cheerleader. I wasn't popular. I wasn't even skinny. I had an acerbic sense of humor, and I had purple hair—yes, it started back in high school. I wrote on the school paper, and I was a member of the poetry club. I was just about as far away from popular as you could get without having some sort of skin condition. Other students—some I thought were friends—told me I'd be really pretty if I lost thirty pounds, and sometimes I'd look in the mirror and tell myself they were right.

Jalen asked me out the fourth week of school. I remember it like it was yesterday. That day, he wore a track-suit that somehow made his body look even more defined than usual, sleek and buttery, aerodynamic and delicious. I saw him before first period, across the quad, and I sat down and opened a book. Instead of reading, I watched him talk to the other Aycees and then walk, slowly, sexily, to his locker. He might have seen me stare.

That day, I wore a skirt that was a little shorter than I was comfortable with, especially since it rode up my thighs so much. I also noticed, with some distaste, that my thighs weren't getting any smaller, and combined with having to get all new bras over the summer that were one cup size larger, I wasn't feeling very good about my body. I'd worn a new dressy white half Oxford shirt that at least was flattering to my larger boobs, but all in all, it hadn't been a good day for my self-esteem.

I'd just walked out of AP Physics when Jalen stopped me. I was a little shocked because he and I had been in the same art class junior year, but other than that we barely knew each other. I wouldn't have been surprised if he hadn't even known my name.

But he'd looked at me with those soulful brown eyes. "Hey, Rachel, can I talk to you a second?"

"Oh. Hi, Jalen." Uh-oh. Maybe he *had* seen me stare at him that morning. "Sure, I guess so. What's up?"

"Would you like to go to a movie with me on Friday night?"

It was the last thing I expected to hear come out of his mouth. "A movie? Uh, like you're asking me on a date?"

His perfect expression faltered, and in that moment, I realized that was exactly what he was doing. Panic flashed in his eyes, and I couldn't believe that he was *nervous*. And he thought I was about to turn him down.

I quickly recovered. "Aren't you already dating Alicia Parker?"

"Oh," he said, and his shoulders relaxed. "No. I mean, we were, but she and I broke up a couple weeks ago."

My guard went up again. Jalen could have easily been lying about the breakup. I'd seen plenty of movies where this was just the sort of practical joke an attractive high school senior would play on a nerdy girl. I narrowed my eyes and stared at his face, searching for some sort of clue that would reveal his true motive.

"What?" he asked. He reached up a tentative hand to his mouth. "Do I—"

"No, no," I said. "I was trying to figure out if you were serious."

He set his jaw. "Listen, if you're not into me, that's cool. You don't have to—"

"Come off it, Jalen," I said. "Every girl at this school is into you. Well, every straight girl, anyway. So why me? Did you lose a bet?"

"Lose a bet?"

"Yeah, you know, I'm"— I almost said *fat*, but then I

shoved that word back down my throat—"on the school paper. I'm not exactly popular. You usually date the cheerleader type."

He frowned. "That's not true. I don't *normally* date the cheerleader type."

I laughed. "What? Alicia Parker isn't the cheerleader type? She comes to school every day looking like a professional artist just photoshopped her. Thin and glamorous, perfect teeth, lustrous golden curls. Not a cheerleader type?"

"She's not a cheerleader." He paused. "But I get your point."

"I don't look anything like Alicia. I don't talk like her. I'm not interested in the same things. Why would you ask me out if it's not a bet?"

"Damn, Rachel, never mind, if you're going to be like that." He hooked his thumbs around the straps of his backpack and turned away from me.

I felt proud of myself. I wouldn't get played, and, in a moment of triumph, I stared at Jalen Jefferson's fine ass as he started to walk away.

Jalen stopped in his tracks and then spun around to face me. I quickly lifted my gaze to his face. "It's because," he said, "you're—you're cool. And funny, but not like goofy or insulting."

I stepped closer to him. "And you're asking me out because I'm funny?"

"Maybe I'm asking you out for a lot of reasons." He tried to keep his eyes focused on my face but they dipped down, taking in my body.

Oh wow. He might *like* the way I look. True, I had a reputation for being smart. And for being a smart-ass. Some guys are turned on by that, I know, but I didn't think Jalen Jefferson would be one of them. If it was my curves he was also interested in, that was okay too.

Though I didn't want to hear the rumblings at school if Jalen Jefferson, handsome stud athlete, dumped magazine-cover-worthy Alicia Parker for the sharp-tongued and over-weight Rachel Constantine.

All right, all right, fine. "Overweight" was not a word that my best friend Elaine liked me to use. *Curvy.* I could still shop at regular clothing stores, just on the double-digit side of things. But Elaine didn't understand. No one had ever been cruel to her about her weight. Trim, athletic Elaine never dreaded the swimming portion of PE, at least not the way I did. The snickers, the cruel comments disguised underneath coughs, especially with the guys, were the worst. When the principal found the popular guys spreading around a *Who Would You Do* list, I'm sure I wasn't on it. But you can bet Alicia Parker with the flawless alabaster skin and the perfect blonde tresses was at the tippy-top.

If you were to pressure me into it, I'd admit to having a pretty face. I also suppose that if Jalen was the kind of guy who liked big boobs and a big butt—a curvy girl, in other words—I'd be on *his Who Would You Do* list. His not-quite-subtle-enough once-over told me that I might have made his top five. But high school is cruel enough a place without having to worry about the popular boys making fat jokes about you, even if you're just curvy.

I studied Jalen's face, and found no trace of malice or joking. In fact, he still had a little nervousness under the façade of bravado.

"Yeah, okay," I said. "That new Quentin Tarantino movie is coming out this weekend. I wouldn't mind seeing that."

"You like Tarantino?"

I nodded. "I even wrote my English lit term paper on *Pulp Fiction* last semester. I compared it to *Macbeth*."

"Wait—you *what?*"

"I compared it to *Macbeth*. Not the whole play, but a section of it."

"Who's the Macbeth character in *Pulp Fiction*? Vincent Vega?"

I elbowed Jalen. "Oh, you're familiar with *Macbeth*?"

"Hey, just because I play sports doesn't mean that's all I talk about. I read Shakespeare." He softened his gaze and then reached out and touched my shoulder like it was no big deal and wouldn't make me melt right there. "So tell me more about this crazy essay of yours."

I swallowed hard and tried to concentrate on his eyes. "Marsellus Wallace is Macbeth."

"Marsellus Wallace? Does that mean Mia is Lady Macbeth?"

"Yep."

"And what does that make Bruce Willis? Macduff?"

I nod, impressed. "Oh, you *do* know the play."

"I *told* you, I like Shakespeare." He smiled—I swear the hallway brightened by a few hundred lumens—and then he squinted hard. "But Bruce Willis's French girlfriend doesn't get killed by Marsellus Wallace's soldiers or anything. She gets to stay in the motel while all that crap is going on."

I tapped my forehead. "No, but he does have to abandon his true love—boxing."

"Hmm, interesting." Jalen tilted his head. "I always

figured he loved his girlfriend way more than he loved boxing."

"Yeah, I know, it doesn't totally hold up. But it was a lot easier than writing how *Reservoir Dogs* was like *A Midsummer Night's Dream*."

That cracked Jalen up. He put a hand in front of his mouth. Then he gave me an appraising look, kind of like he was seeing me for the first time. "You know, I wouldn't have pegged you for a Tarantino fan."

"And I wouldn't have pegged you for a Shakespeare fan." I was dying to ask him some more questions about Shakespeare *and* Tarantino, but it was between classes and we didn't have much time.

"So, uh, how's Friday? We'll go to dinner and then maybe we can catch the new Tarantino movie around seven thirty?"

I nodded. "That sounds great."

I floated to my next class, but I could barely wait for it to be over. I had to tell Elaine that Jalen Jefferson, yes, *the* Jalen Jefferson, had asked me out. The seconds seemed to drag by. The lecture was particularly awful and cringe-inducing. Time went in slow-motion.

I rushed out of the classroom as soon as the bell rang and practically ran over to Elaine's locker. "Oh my God, oh my God, oh my God, Elaine, you'll never *believe* what happened."

"Jalen Jefferson asked you out before last period," Elaine said. She fluttered her eyelashes at me and smirked.

Shit. News travels fast.

"Uh—yeah." I kept talking a mile a minute. "I mean, I know he's popular and super tasty, but I'm not excited *just* because he's gorgeous. He and I talked about Tarantino movies and Shakespeare. He knew that Bruce Willis was Macduff."

"Bruce Willis was who now?"

"Never mind. It's just that he's *smart*, Elaine. We might have a good time."

Elaine was quiet.

"Elaine, what is it?" My eyes widened. "Oh no, *you* don't have a crush on him, do you?"

She shook her head. "No, that's not it. I mean, yeah, *everybody* has some sort of crush on him. But I just don't know."

I knew that look in her eyes.

She was worried about me.

I felt like I'd been hit by a truck. I swallowed hard and blinked a few times so I could get ahold of myself and not start crying in the middle of the hall. "Crap." My voice broke, but I blundered on. "I knew he was just messing with my head. Great. Now everyone will laugh at me." I took a deep breath and put my hands on my hips. "What was it? Did he lose a bet? Was it some sort of joke on me? Whether or not I'd actually believe that Jalen would seriously ask a fat girl out? God, I'm such an idiot."

"You are *not* fat," Elaine said, seething.

"Well, why else would they fuck with me like that?"

"I don't—" Elaine shook her head, exasperated, then pulled two textbooks out of her locker. "Hold on, let me get my stuff and we'll go over there."

"Over where?"

"Around the corner of the building. Over by the rock garden."

"We'll be late to the cafeteria."

"Yes." Elaine stuffed her sweatshirt in her backpack.

"They might be all out of—"

"Oh, for crying out loud, Rachel. This is important." Elaine slammed her locker shut and grabbed my hand, hauling me around the corner. There was a sidewalk leading to the rock garden and then the iron gate that surrounded the school's campus.

"Okay, okay, Elaine. I get it. They're trying to make the geeky weird poetry girl with purple hair into a laughingstock. It's not worth arguing with anyone about. I'll tell Jalen the next time I see him that I'm going out of town with my folks this weekend. It's no big deal."

"No," Elaine said. She lowered her voice. I could barely hear her above the fan. "That's not it."

My heart leaped, but I tried to stay on an even keel. I squinted at Elaine. "What? Then what's the problem?"

"The problem? Do you not know who Jalen hangs out with? You're not, well, *cool* enough to hang out with them. Alicia and Jalen still hang out with the all the Aycees."

I made a retching noise.

Elaine ignored me. "You know that clique is like fuckin' British royalty. Aycees only date other Aycees. If Jalen starts dating you, there will be hell to pay. You don't deserve that hell landing on your head."

I rolled my eyes. "Jesus. I hate drama. I wouldn't be in the Aycees if you *paid* me. So what? It's not like Jalen and I are boyfriend-girlfriend. It's one date. I don't even know if I'll like hanging out with him. I mean, I know he *says* he likes Tarantino movies and Shakespeare plays, and he doesn't like talking about sports, but come on. I'm not taking any of what he says at face value." I stopped for a moment. Was there a way he could have gotten all that information about what I like from other sources, or was it genuine?

Oh, of course. I wrote for the school paper, and I'd written articles about the latest Tarantino movie. I also reviewed the school's last attempt at the Bard's work, a terrible production of *A Midsummer Night's Dream* that whitewashed everything edgy or funny from the play. What we ended up with was a tame production no one would find remotely offensive or, unfortunately, interesting. Jalen could have gone over our back issues online and done his homework to make sure he knew about Tarantino and Shakespeare.

So maybe his interests *weren't* genuine.

But—hold on. Research like that would actually require *effort*, and Jalen wouldn't study my likes and dislikes just to make fun of me. Maybe he *did* like me.

Or maybe he really *was* into Tarantino and Shakespeare.

Elaine shook her head. "You better watch your back. I had Alicia in my last class. She's already saying the only reason Jalen's going out with you is because you let guys titty-fuck you on the first date."

I burst out laughing. "Really? That's what she says?"

Elaine nodded.

"Why in the world would she say that?"

"She *says* you came out of that adult store over on Corning Avenue a couple months ago."

I grinned.

"Wait—you were actually *there*?"

"Sure."

"Why in the world would you go in?"

"I bought myself a vibrator for my eighteenth birthday."

Elaine flinched as if I'd socked her in the arm. "You *what?*"

I rolled my eyes. "I might still be a virgin, but that doesn't mean I can't have a good time." I winked. "Besides, how will I tell Jalen where to put his tongue if I don't know what feels good?"

She stared out past my shoulder, into space. "Wow. You had the guts to go into that place and actually buy a vibrator."

I laughed. "Of course I did. Where else would I get it? Order it off the web? No way. First of all, I don't have a credit card. Second of all, I'd be *mortified* if my parents got the package before I did." I paused. "But just because Alicia saw me walking out of the adult store doesn't automatically mean I like having my boobs fucked. That doesn't even make sense."

"No. She never said why she thought that. She must be jealous of your boobs."

"What? Get out of here."

Elaine shrugged. "Lots of girls are jealous of your boobs."

I blinked hard. "You've got to be kidding."

"Oh, come on, you must notice the stares from all the guys. Especially when you wear the red sweater you had on the first day of school. Or that sparkly aqua tank top you wore last Thursday."

"No way. I mean, yeah, I've noticed the looks, but I just thought all guys are perverted sex clowns."

It was Elaine's turn to laugh. "Well, yes, they *are* all perverted sex clowns, but they all want to make that sparkly top their clown car."

"What?"

"That means they all want to get inside—oh, never mind."

"Hmm." I nodded, looking down at my outfit. Yes, the fitted half Oxford shirt *did* flatter my torso. My black capri pants were tight around my hips—my big butt made *everything* tight around my hips—and fitted down my legs. I did have nice calves. I know that's probably a weird thing to say, and an even weirder thing to think boys would notice, but nevertheless, it was true. They were shapely, and especially if I was wearing heels, my calves looked *great*. Heels also made my butt look sexier. I didn't know what it was. Maybe it was the way I had to stand in heels that changed the angle of my pelvis. I'd caught more than one perverted sex clown staring at my ass when I wore heels.

"Did you hear if Jalen thinks my sparkly top would make a good clown car?"

"I know that *I've* caught him looking. And if I caught him looking, he must be doing it an awful lot."

"Interesting," I said, tapping my finger to my chin.

"I say this to warn you," Elaine said. "You don't want to make an enemy of Alicia. She's too powerful in this school."

"I could take Alicia."

"Maybe in a fight," Elaine said, "but she'd *kill* you in terms of social reputation."

I scoffed. "As if I have a social reputation to damage."

"Better no reputation than a bad one. She could get a lie out so easily. That you've got some sort of STD. Or that you're screwing a couple of guys behind Jalen's back. She could get especially nasty if she wants him back."

"Do you know who broke up with who?"

"Well, I heard Alicia say that she broke up with Jalen

because he was too immature. He didn't know what he wanted." She paused. "She also said that he was always looking at
another girl when they were together." Elaine pitched her
voice up and made it breathy, a pretty good imitation of
Alicia. "'I mean, *I'm* obviously the most beautiful girl at
Montrose High. I don't know what he sees in her. She's not
even *pretty*, she walks in with her dumb purple hair and it's
like he can't take his eyes off her.'"

My eyes widened. "Wait."

"Oh, uh, yeah. Sorry. Jalen's liked you for a while. I guess
Alicia had finally had enough. She knows he likes you,
Rachel. She's not happy about it."

I was silent.

"She's pissed off at you already. You're the reason she
broke up with Jalen. And if the two of you start going out,
it'll make things rough for her. That means she'll make
things rough for you, too."

I sighed. "She's already done it. I bet she was the one
who glued my locker shut last week. In room 28, there's an
econ class in there before journalism, and Alicia's in that
class. I bet she broke my camera." I thought for a moment.
"That was about two weeks ago. How long ago did they
break up?"

"The day after the Homecoming Rally."

I paused, counting the days, and then I burst out
laughing.

"What is it?"

"The day after the Homecoming Rally we were having
that heat wave, right? I wore that white tank top."

Elaine's eyes danced. "Oh yes, the famous titty tank top."

"Yeah. The one that Mrs. García told me to cover up.

She even brought a sweatshirt from the lost and found. I don't see what the big deal is. I wore a bra. It's not like you could see my nipples or anything."

Elaine shrugged. "They told me to go home and change my skirt because it was too short, but when I did the ruler test it was an inch longer than it needed to be. They told me that it was distracting some of the boys, so I had to go home and change anyway."

"People suck," I said.

"Yes." Elaine nodded. "So what are you going to do about Alicia?"

I thought for a moment. "Maybe I can set up some cameras or something. Try to catch her in the act."

"I don't know," Elaine said. "Alicia sure seems like she can do no wrong at this school."

"Maybe she's fucking the principal."

We both laughed and walked to the cafeteria.

A LITTLE REUNION

Upper management wouldn't let Jalen come back Monday night, which pissed me off, especially since he not only saved the account in London but got them to invest in a new offering. They signed a purchase order for over two million dollars.

We have a Skype call together on Monday night. It's almost eleven o'clock, which means nearly seven in the morning for him on Tuesday. He's dressed in his navy pinstripe suit, all ready for work. Even though I'm super horny, and I want to beg him to talk dirty to me while I finger myself, I don't even bring up the possibility of video chat sex. It's clear that he's on his way out of his hotel and worried about what his boss will say.

"I'm sorry," I say, rubbing my palm along the inside of my thighs. "I hope everything will be okay."

"Me too." He glances at his watch. "Okay, I have to get going. Love you."

"Love you too."

He smiles and the call disconnects.

I get ready for bed, but I toss and turn for about half an hour before finally falling asleep. Then the next thing I know, my eyes are wide open.

I look at the clock on the bedside table. It's a quarter after two in the morning.

I roll on my back. This travel schedule is killing our connection. I might have to alter my schedule when he gets home. The months stretch out before us, and lately Jalen has become more and more of a shell of himself, and suddenly sadness overwhelms me. It's worse than our first three years together, when we weren't officially boyfriend and girlfriend. During that time, we drove to see each other as often as we could on the weekends, whenever I had class canceled on a Friday, or whenever he had a weekend that wasn't sucked up by basketball.

The tears leak out of my eyes, and I roll over and put my face in the pillow. I cry silently, and my shoulders begin to shake. If I had gone through my whole life never knowing the kind of love and intimacy that I had with Jalen, I might not grieve like this over what we've lost, but I feel empty inside. It's like this job has sucked out his passion for everything, including me.

I know things are bad because I don't even want to call him on Skype and tell him how upset I am over everything. He would be understanding and he'd feel awful about it, but there's nothing for him to do. It's not like he can magically hop on a jet home, or suddenly Roger will tell him he doesn't have to go to Zurich anymore. It's not like my complaining will be a boner pill that would suddenly get him to make the slow, tender love to me that I need, followed by the rough, hard fucking that my body craves.

I can't believe that this is happening to me. I thought moving to Sacramento would be fantastic for us. I'd have a steady, less stressful, public-service job, great benefits, and an excellent option for maternity leave when Jalen and I got pregnant. Jalen not only made a lot more money in this new position, but the cost of living was lower than Orange County. Everything was lining up for us.

And then the realities of Jalen's job hit.

I know a lot of couples go through stuff like this, and I feel idiotic that I'm so devastated over a stupid *boy*. I've always been able to make friends. I did it with two women at work, and even though both of them have left, I'm sure I can make friends again. Maybe try harder to get to know some other women in the book club or rock climbing meet-ups.

Or maybe I can get into a writing group.

I almost start to laugh when I picture myself reading my werejaguar story out loud in front of a shocked and disapproving audience, talking about the half man, half cat sliding his cock in and out of my wet, dripping pussy, screaming his name during orgasm.

And then, out of nowhere, a barrage of negative images slam into my brain. My lonely nights when Jalen isn't here. A few of the women on our cul-de-sac are either pregnant or have infants. Most of them are younger than me, too. Does anyone care about the smutty unicorn sex scenes that I write to fill the time? To while away the hours of my empty life? It's not like anyone is reading these. I'm not sending them to agents or trying to publish them. Who'd take me seriously anyway?

God, Rachel, you're so stupid. You're stupid for thinking Jalen could ever love you. You're stupid for thinking that he's not enjoying being away from you every time he gets on that plane to Zurich. You're stupid for thinking you're more attractive than Alicia. That Jalen would ever want a baby with you.

Oh my God, I have to get out of here.

I try to control my breathing as I jump out of bed and pee, and then I pull open my drawer and dress in a workout shirt and sweatpants. We belong to a twenty-four-hour gym down the street. Jalen keeps saying that he can't go anymore because of his travel schedule, and I haven't been in a few weeks, so we shouldn't keep paying for membership, but right now, I need it. I run downstairs and go out to my car. I drive to the gym, the voices still pinging in my head, back and forth, repeating all the things about myself I hate or I'm scared of.

The gym isn't anywhere near deserted at 2:45 a.m., although it's full of gym rats, men in muscle shirts or slender-backed tank tops, and groups of two women scattered here and there, spotting each other on the free weights, or taking turns on the machines.

The cardio area is crowded, with only a couple of bikes and one elliptical machine available. I get on the elliptical and start moving, and my field of vision narrows until all I can see in front of me is the control panel. I move the resistance higher and then close my eyes.

What the hell am I going to do?

Jalen fortunately makes his nonstop flight on Tuesday, Heathrow to SFO, leaving at four in the afternoon London time, and he sends me a text from the plane just before take-off. I get his message just as I get to my desk.

He's scheduled to arrive in San Francisco that evening about a quarter after seven, and then he'll go through customs, get his luggage, take the shuttle to long-term parking, and drive over a hundred miles home. I calculate the time and expect him somewhere between eleven and midnight. And he'll be worn out.

I check my emails and respond to a couple of urgent requests, and then I have a planning meeting for an hour. Preoccupied with thoughts of Jalen coming home, I feel like a mocha might help me focus. So I go around the corner to Temple Coffee on 25th and H Street.

I stand in line and order a medium mocha, and decide to order it in, getting it in one of their fancy ceramic mugs rather than a paper cup. I don't usually take twenty minutes away from work in the middle of the morning, but I'm a little ahead on the project.

I watch the barista carefully pour the steamed milk in the mug, making a flower shape with the foam, and then she dusts cocoa powder over the top.

Delightful.

Taking a seat at one of the small tables, I take a big loud sip of the mocha and glance at the woman in the chair.

She's staring back at me.

Holy shit.

It's Alicia.

I narrow my eyes, but it's Alicia who speaks first.

"Rachel Constantine?"

"Alicia Parker?"

She holds up her hand so I can see her huge diamond

engagement ring and her wedding band. "It's Alicia *Hawthorne* now." Her smug smile chills my heart just as much as it did in high school.

I hold up my left hand too, with the significantly smaller diamond. "And I'm Rachel *Jefferson* now."

"Jefferson?" Her eyes crinkle at the corners and she frowns.

"Yes, Alicia. As in Jalen Jefferson."

"You *married* Jalen?"

I nodded.

"But—you couldn't even—"

I shrug. "I know. Not sure why it didn't happen in high school. We wound up dating after graduating college, got married, and moved up here."

She leans back and an icy calm descends over her. "That's wonderful to hear, Rachel."

"What are *you* doing in Sacramento, Alicia?"

"Oh, Allan's family lives over in Folsom, and I was offered an excellent position at a financial firm downtown." She smiles mirthlessly. "I love this place. You could set your watch by my ten-o'clock extra-large half-caf quad latte."

"Jalen and I had no idea you even lived in California. It's crazy that you work downtown."

"Two years in April. Beckett Equity. You might have heard of us?"

I nod. They famously brokered the big Q-Merit deal three years ago. Not only did the deal rescue Q-Merit from bankruptcy, they brought another ten thousand tech jobs to Sacramento. It would be tough to find a person in the valley who *hadn't* heard of Beckett.

"It's a difficult job, of course, but I love it. My indexes routinely beat the S&P 500 by several percent every year."

I nod. "Jalen's at an investment firm too. International finance."

"What firm?"

"Woodward Reynolds."

Alicia's smile turns tight-lipped. "That's an excellent firm. He must be doing well. They're owned by a Swiss company, aren't they?"

"Not anymore. He just found out that the Swiss sold them off again."

"Ah. Well, if he's hitting his numbers, I'm sure not much will change." She takes a sip of her complicated latte, and then sets it down, a smug smile touching the corners of her mouth. "It's an excellent industry to be in, of course. I do well enough that Allan can stay home with the children. It's such a relief when the kids can be raised by a parent, don't you think?"

I shrug.

She rubs her hands together. "Do you work outside the home?"

Holy shit, Alicia hasn't changed a bit. She's sitting there, calculating what she can say that will get under my skin the most. And since I'm caught off guard, I'm reactive instead of proactive. I have to change my tactics.

"I do. I'm a project manager at the California State Infrastructure Board."

"Ah. Public service. How"—Alicia clicks her tongue almost imperceptibly—"*noble*."

"I don't know about that, but I enjoy the work."

"You enjoy the work." Alicia tilts her head. "Hah. Interesting. So, where's Jalen?"

"At work," I said, and then I debate whether to say where he really is. "Flying home today, actually." I try to give the words the same overcoating of smugness that Alicia has practically patented.

"Oh." Alicia cocks her head to the side. "Does he travel a lot? That must be hard."

Dammit, after not seeing me for over a decade, Alicia found my trigger in less than five minutes.

I force a smile on my face, sip my mocha, and I don't respond.

"So," Alicia says, "if I remember correctly, you and Jalen had that *disastrous* first date in high school. What happened? Did you finally put out as soon as you found out you were going to the same college?" She laughed, as if she and I have an inside joke about it—as if she isn't trying to slut-shame me.

I smile sweetly. "Oh no, we didn't go to the same school."

"Really? I guess I just assumed you went to the same state school he did." Alicia's voice is flat and low.

I debate how much to tell her. I know she's fishing for information, but I bet she'd hate it if I told her about Jalen and me in college.

"I went to UC Irvine, but Arrowhead U is only about an hour away. I'd drive down and visit Jalen now and again. Drive to the lake, stuff like that. Lake Arrowhead's got a couple of beaches and it's nice and warm all the way through October."

"I'll bet," she said drily, and I know I've pushed one of her buttons. I can see it in her eyes. She's thinking of us all on the beach, but Jalen completely ignoring her, and unable to take his eyes off me. Imagine her anger if I told her about how I gave Jalen a blow job in the Western Philosophy section on the fifth floor of the Arrowhead library.

It *still* drives her crazy that Jalen never preferred her supposedly magazine-cover worthy body better than mine. That's my trump card with her. She can have a perfect life with perfect children and a perfect job, but she'll never forgive me for Jalen's head swiveling toward me in my tight red sweater in the corridors all those years ago.

I take a drink of my mocha and appraise Alicia over the top of my cup. The years have, unfortunately, been kind to her. She's thirty-five, the same age I am, but she looks like she could pass for midtwenties. Maybe. Her eyes might give her away. Not that she has crow's feet or bags, but it's her eyes themselves don't have the innocence of a twenty-five-year-old. She's seen some dark things, and I can sense the mistrust in her gaze.

"Do you and Jalen have children?"

"Oh. No, we don't."

Alicia clicked her tongue. "You've been together since college, but you don't have kids?"

I don't correct Alicia on her timeline.

"You better get going, girl. You're playing with Father Time. Pretty soon you won't be able to have any."

I press my lips together. This isn't one of those things where I can tell Alicia about our problems having kids or how expensive IVF is. She's already gloating about her career and two kids and a stay-at-home husband, lording her life success over me. So even though I married the man she was attached to in high school—if a succubus like her could even recognize love as an emotion—she has it all and I don't. That's a trough she could go back to over and over, and I don't want to give her that power.

So I laugh, the heartiest guffaw I can muster. "I don't know what the fuss is, frankly. Not being able to sleep in for six or eight years? Having to hide all the sex toys you and your husband play together with? Every time you get on top of him, you just go, 'oh my God, what if my kids walk in?'"

Alicia's smile freezes on her face.

"Don't get me wrong." I lean forward and pat her hand. "A lot of people think kids are their legacy. They have some sort of bond they can't get with anyone else." I sit back and take another sip of my mocha. "But then I read some story about a mother with four kids driving off a cliff on purpose and killing them all, or drowning them all in the bathtub. I mean, how horrible!"

Alicia blinks.

"Maybe the idea of having it all is a dangerous myth, meant to keep women subjugated, turning against each other." I look up in Alicia's eyes. "Know what I mean?"

Alicia's mouth is smiling, but it's the only part of her face not full of fury.

The door opens and a man, wearing a front-facing baby carrier, enters. He's short, maybe a couple of inches shorter than I am, and his dark curly hair and glasses frame a face with a kind smile but hard brown eyes. The baby in the carrier is absolutely beautiful. He's got a big round head, Alicia's green eyes, and an adorable toothless grin. He can't be more than six months old, and Alicia already is back to her Cosmo-model size. *Bitch.*

The man, presumably Alicia's husband, walks through

the maze of tables to her. "Roscoe made it to preschool, no problem."

Roscoe? Do they have a child or a dachshund?

"Sorry," Alicia says, "Roscoe was fighting me so much this morning."

"He's calmed down and they're fine now." He looks at me and smiles. "And who's this?"

Alicia stands up and grabs her purse. "Rachel, this is my husband, Allan Hawthorne. Allan, this is Rachel Constantine."

"Your baby is the cutest thing ever," I say, "and it's Jefferson now, not Constantine."

"Right, Jefferson." Alicia cocks her head. "She and I went to high school together."

"Ah," Allan says, holding out his hand. "Jefferson—hmm. Alicia has told me about an ex-boyfriend she had. Wasn't his last name Jefferson?"

"Jalen Jefferson," Alicia says, and then slaps a grin on her face. I can tell it's only for her husband's benefit. "Turns out Jalen and Rachel got married."

"Congratulations," Allan says warmly. He turns to Alicia. "Come along now, dear. I'll walk you back to work before I head home."

"It was great seeing you again, Rachel," Alicia says in a singsong voice, dripping with hatred. "We'll have to get the families together soon for a good old-fashioned backyard barbecue."

"Sure," I say. "Don't be a stranger."

"I have a feeling we'll be seeing each other soon enough." Alicia spins on her heel and walks out.

Allan stares after her a moment, the baby yawning.

"Well," he says, "I feel I must apologize for my wife's behavior."

I almost tell him that I'm used to it, but bite my tongue.

Neither of us gave the other any of our contact information. No phone number, no email address, no instant messenger account invite. I suppose she could find me on some social media account, but I'm sure as hell not planning to search for her. I have a feeling she'd be glad to never see me again.

Their baby is awfully cute, though. I hope he doesn't get his mother's personality.

THE FORKED TONGUE

*T*hat night, I come home to an empty house, like I do every night when Jalen is in Zurich.

I can't get the conversation with Alicia out of my head, and I debate what to do about it. I open the refrigerator and shut it almost as quickly. I pull my phone out of my purse, but who am I supposed to call? I can't talk to my parents about this, and no one from work would understand—they'd have to know Alicia.

Aha! Elaine, of course. I look at the clock on the wall of the kitchen. It's almost nine o'clock in New York. She'll still be awake.

She answers on the third ring. "Oh my God, is that Rachel Jefferson calling me?"

"Hey, Elaine. Sorry. It's been a long time."

"Don't worry about it. I just got home from work."

"At nine?"

"It's crazy. When I started this job, I thought I'd keep bankers' hours, but nope. The world markets never sleep."

She laughs lightly. "But I don't have to tell *you* about working long days. Is that app coming out any time soon?"

I stammer. "Oh, actually, no. The company went under. Have we really not talked in two years?"

"Wow. I should be paying closer attention to your social media." There's rustling in the background. Perhaps she's getting more comfortable on the couch. "What's up? Everything okay?"

"Yes, well, kind of."

"Did something happen with Jalen?"

I hesitate, and then I tell Elaine about all the travel. How when Jalen first transferred into this job, we thought it would be great. How his higher salary allowed us to afford the IVF, how he was loving and attentive and always home on the weekends.

"But then the app company laid *everybody* off," I said.

"Everyone?"

"I mean, they paid below market value anyway. I was there for the stock options. But I didn't even get a severance package."

"What did you do?"

"I went to work for the state. Public infrastructure. I'm helping to put a new bridge over the Sacramento river."

"Oh, that's cool," Elaine says. "Something tangible. I bet you like working on that better than a gaming app anyway."

"Hell, yes, I do." I kick my shoes off and plop on the couch as well. "And the hours are way better. No more getting home at eleven at night or working every weekend."

"Are you liking Sacramento okay?"

I hesitate.

"Uh-oh. Is this why you're calling me? I thought you were making friends there."

"I had a couple of coworker friends. But one of them moved away, and one of them had a baby and I haven't talked to her since."

"Oh, I'm sorry, Rachel. But Jalen's there, right?"

"I was getting to that. It's actually the reason I'm calling." I hesitate and sigh. "He's traveling all the time for work. He's in Zurich for over half the month."

"Wow, Zurich? Like, Switzerland?"

"Yeah," I say miserably. "And it's awful. It's like we've lost our connection."

We talk for another forty-five minutes about Jalen traveling, and then she complains about her perpetual singleness and her ticking biological clock.

"But," I say, "you'll never guess who I saw today."

"Oh, that must be a teacher or something. Is it the hot student teacher from sophomore English?"

"No."

"I wonder what he's doing now," she muses quietly.

"I saw Alicia."

"What? Alicia *Parker* Alicia?"

"She's married now, but yes."

"What's she doing in Sacramento?" Elaine asks, her voice rising.

"High-powered job at Beckett Financial."

"What? *She* works at Beckett?"

And I relate our conversation, as close to word for word as I can remember, and especially highlighting the bitchy undertones.

Elaine is quiet for a moment. Then she takes a breath

and holds it for a second before asking, "Did she *actually* say, 'We'll be seeing each other soon enough'?"

"Yep."

"Did it sound like a threat? Or was it just one of those things you say instead of goodbye?"

For a few seconds, I consider this. "I'm not really sure. Her tone wasn't exactly threatening. It was more *amused* than anything."

"I don't like this," Elaine said. "Alicia is not to be trusted."

"I'm not going to trust her with anything," I reply. "And I'm never going into Temple Coffee again at ten o'clock. She can have her alone time with her complicated coffee order."

We shift the conversation to movies, although neither of us has seen anything good recently. I don't mention the dirty stories I write. We promise each other we'll do a better job of keeping in touch and I hang up.

Then, instead of just sitting and waiting for Jalen to come home, I walk into our home office, wake up my laptop, and stare at the words on the page.

Jalen is still the werejaguar, sleek and sexual and powerful, and ready to just take me, make me come like I belong to him. But after I finish the sex scene, I'm not sure where to take the story.

And yes, I know that the preferred term is *werepanther*. (Fun fact: panthers, cougars, mountain lions, jaguars, and pumas are all the same species, says the geeky girl in the poetry club with the purple hair.) But the term feels weird in my head. Besides, I can write anything I want; it's not like I'll be selling the movie rights any time soon.

I'm not one of those people who needs a partner to be

complete. After the startup folded, got involved in a lot of activities in the area, now that I wasn't spending all my time at work. I'd been looking forward to joining the book club, but the other women are awfully uptight. A couple of the other participants look at me warily, as if I'd steal their purses just because I have purple hair. Imagine if they found out my husband was black.

When I first dyed my hair as a freshman in high school, everyone said that it was just a phase. When I meet people for the first time, too, they're often surprised that I've had the same shade of purple—Arctic Amethyst—for twenty years. Now that I'm on the far side of thirty, I'm not sure I'll ever change it. I'll be a purple-haired old lady in a retirement home, and my friends' kids will come visit them and tell me that my purple hair is just a phase.

For one thing, I *really* like it. Back in high school, my purple hair set me apart, even from the other weirdos in Phoenix. I like being able to say to strangers on the phone, "I'll meet you at the food court. I'm the one with purple hair."

About four months ago, right after my coworker Lily and her wife had the baby, I attended a book club meeting. Jalen had left for Zurich the day before, and I was freaking out that after book club, I had nothing planned for the next two weeks except Lean Cuisines for dinner and binge watching *Peaky Blinders*.

That month, our book club discussed one of those literary-minded Jane Austen sequels. (Side rant. Sure, it's okay for society to make fun of *my* Dragon Brothers fan fiction where Vivienne Goodheart and Jacques Eversword get together, but make fan fiction about Elizabeth and Mr. Darcy, and suddenly you've got a full-page spread in the *New York Times Book Review*.)

The book tried too hard to sound smart. Actually, it was perfect for our book club, because a lot of the other women tried too hard to be Stepford wives. I counted the different types of tea sandwiches in the triple-decker serving tray sitting on the glass-and-ironwork coffee table. Six different kinds. All of them tasted like mayonnaise and desperation.

We started discussing the book. A couple of the other women raved about it, showing off their vocabularies, but there wasn't enough conflict, and I didn't care about any of the new characters. Worst of all, at least in my mind, hints of passion-filled moments abounded, but no heat emanated from any of the prose. I remember saying out loud, "Jeez, if I'd written this, we'd at least get to see Mr. Darcy's throbbing cock."

The room went silent and everyone looked at me.

Instead of smiling demurely and trying to back out of that statement, I doubled down. "Oh, come *on*, Robin. You honestly weren't disappointed with the way Chapter Seventeen ended? I wanted to see that seething rage that was just under the surface with Darcy's housemaid get channeled into some hardcore fucking with the stable boy. I wanted to see her get on top of him and ride him until she screamed so loud from the pleasure she scared the horses. Sex so good it causes a stampede. Now *that's* something to tell your grandkids."

Robin fumbled her words.

Suzanne said, "That is *hardly* appropriate, Rachel."

"I'll go refill my zin," I said, grabbing a sadness-and-butter tea sandwich. "Anyone else?"

When I came back from the showcase-worthy kitchen with a full glass in one hand and the rest of the bottle of overpriced Chateau le Boulet in the other, Mr. Darcy and the stable boy were no longer running through my head. Instead, I planned to take that Dragon Brothers fan fiction I wrote in high school and really amp up the sex scenes between Vivienne and Jacques. For those of you who haven't read the Dragon Brothers series, Jacques is the evil dude. He even has a forked tongue, as if the other imagery wasn't obvious enough.

I sat down with my full glass and fantasized about getting oral from a guy with a forked tongue. I paid little attention to the rest of the discussion.

When book club ended that night, I got a ride home from Robin, since I'd refilled my wineglass five times. Robin made polite chitchat with me but I wouldn't be getting a place on her Christmas card list. I got home at eight o'clock, still with forked-tongue cunnilingus on my mind. I settled my drunk ass at my desk and woke up the computer.

If the FBI ever gets ahold of my PC, they'll be either disgusted or aroused by my search history. Maybe both. The night I came home from book club is the night my browser history took a turn for the perverse.

I searched for *forked tongues,* and I went down the rabbit hole of extreme body modification. One of those modifications is getting one's tongue surgically split—it's preferred name is *tongue bifurcation.* Either super interesting or kinda gross, or both, depending on how you feel about these things. It's both for me. But my curiosity won out. It was for *science*.

Strangely, though, the articles I found focused mostly on the occult meanings, or of the medical complications that a couple of people faced. For instance, it's a reversible process, but reversing the bifurcation is more painful than splitting it in the first place. Kind of like tattoos, I guess. One online news source had a special Friday the 13th edition and tongue bifurcation was in an article called *The 13 Most Extreme Body Mods*.

Maybe it wasn't weird that just about everything was about secret occult meanings and medical issues, but for me, I expected a lot more articles on the sexual possibilities of a forked tongue. Seriously, search for the most mundane thing you can think of, then add *sex* after the search term—and boom! There's a whole PornProfs channel dedicated to it. Surely *someone* has reported on the sexual uses of a bifurcated tongue.

When the search engines failed me, I went directly to some online porn sites, but the few-and-far-between video results led to broken links. One looked especially intriguing, too, promising a point of view from the woman who was having a guy with a bifurcated tongue performing cunnilingus on her. That's the way it was phrased too —*performing cunnilingus*. I was worried it'd be too clinical, but that would also mean better-than-average camera work, where one could clearly see the tongue in all its glory.

Unfortunately, the only video I found was a really bad porno where Satan was leading an orgy. A bunch of devils were all sexing up a fake-boobed blonde dressed in flowing all-white gauzy robes. She had a halo made of cheap-looking gold tinsel. Satan was the only one with a forked tongue, though, and he was just egging the other devils on, not doing anything at all with his bifurcation.

I did watch the scene twice—it was kind of hot in spite of its lack of what I was searching for—but I didn't find out anything more about forked-tongue cunnilingus. I also found a discussion forum on the subject, but it was largely hypothetical, with each side, pro and con, typing out an argument worthy of an elementary school playground.

> XUZI75: *its supper hott*
> PORKPIEHAT: *no it's not it's disgusting*
> XUZI75: *your the 1 whose disgutsing*
> PORKPIEHAT: *your mom is disgusting and you need to learn to spell*

I did, however, starting about eleven thirty, write a couple of really great sex scenes for my Dragon Brothers fanfic. In my story, each side of the tongue had independent movement, a topic lightly debated in the forum. In addition to the bifurcated tongue, Jacques Eversword also—after the angelic Vivienne Goodheart orgasmed for the third time, her juices exploding all over his face—grew a prehensile tail.

After I'd written three pages, I found myself surprisingly sober but *very* horny. I went to bed shortly thereafter, taking a vibrator with me, and spent the next hour fantasizing about Jalen growing a tail and teasing my nipples with it as each side of his forked tongue worked feverishly to run in small circles around my clit.

I was twenty minutes late to work the next day, but I had

the most productive morning I'd had in months. Jalen even commented on how refreshed I looked on our lunchtime Skype call.

Ever since then, whenever Jalen is traveling, I've written a scene or two every night in my "stories." I don't really know what else to call them, although I'm afraid I sound like an old lady following soap operas.

I abandoned the forked-tongue premise and Dragon Brothers fan fiction after about a week, and I started a brand-new story, *The Princess and the Unicorn*. I didn't really have any idea what I would write, but it was like the energy and ideas came directly from the Muse into my fingers, bypassing my brain. Probably because my brain wasn't the body part the inspiration was coming from.

The stories are here to keep me company. I've worked on three stories in the last six months. They're a weird length—way too short for a novel but too long for a short story.

When I get home after having that odd conversation at Temple Coffee with Alicia, I look at the clock—Jalen's already on the plane. Mm. When he gets home tonight, I wonder what things he might do to me? Maybe tonight he won't be too exhausted. Maybe he'll get a few hours' sleep on the plane. Maybe he'll get into bed and we'll make love, sweetly and tenderly. Or maybe he'll rip my panties off and put his hard cock in my wet, needy pussy, whispering in my ear what a dirty girl I am.

It will be another four or five hours until Jalen gets home. I walk upstairs to my PC and wake it up, and then I go into my stories folder and find the latest version of *The Princess and the Unicorn*.

I remember the night I began to write this one, too, and

all the emotions that brought up. It's probably why I continue to write, even as Jalen's business trips keep extending.

Jalen and I both feature prominently in the story, too. Yes, it's a little immature, but it does the job....

THE PRINCESS AND THE UNICORN

 $\mathcal{L}$ ong ago, in a faraway kingdom, Princess Rachel was the only heir to the throne.

Her parents, the king and queen, were kind and gentle, but they worried about their princess. Her security was not only important to the family, but to the entire kingdom. So they decided to sequester the princess in the royal castle to keep her safe. Knowing she would one day rule over all the lands as far as the eye could see, Rachel studied attentively with the best writers, healers, scientists, mathematicians, artists, musicians, witches, and seers that her parents brought from the far reaches of their kingdom.

The only area of their kingdom from which they did not seek a teacher was the Forest of Shadows. Rumors were that magical creatures roamed the forest, untamed and unfriendly to humans. People who entered the forest rarely returned, and those who did were never the same and rarely spoke of their adventures. The Forest of Shadows abutted the castle lands, and the king and queen forbade their daughter from entering.

Princess Rachel hungrily consumed all of the training and teachings presented to her. However, while learning sated one need while growing up, the princess had other needs as well. As she grew into adulthood, she began to request more sessions with the handsome scientist who had the chiseled jaw, and took a liking to the lute, often staring at the blond-tressed young man who showed her the complicated fingering. Her lessons were always supervised by her lady's maid, but she noticed that the science and lute lessons were increasingly overseen by her mother, the queen.

So as much as the princess's thirst for knowledge was sated, her desire for more earthly pleasures was not. She would often sneak books from her teachers and by moonlight or candlelight, study the chapters that the teachers skipped over. From her poetry teacher, she thieved a book of love poems whose verses made her breath catch and her knees quiver. From the chisel-jawed scientist, she purloined an anatomy book and spent hours studying the mysteries of the human body. And from the woman who taught her the duties of royalty, she filched a book about her kingdom, and eagerly read the chapters on the Forest of Shadows. Several people had returned speaking of a race of unicorns in the forest—but not the kind, benevolent creatures of myth. Instead, these unicorns were haughty and insolent, treating humans as trespassers, and according to one young woman who'd fled their clutches, they were able to transform into the most beautiful humans she'd ever seen.

Increasingly frustrated by the castle walls as she grew into womanhood, she wondered if she would ever escape the confines of her role, or learn enough about the kingdom she would inherit to be an effective leader.

The day of Princess Rachel's eighteenth birthday dawned sunny and mild, perfect for an outdoor feast. Nobles from across the kingdom came to celebrate with the king and queen. Soon, they all sat at the table, the king and queen at each end, ready for the food to arrive.

The princess, who was seated at the center, stood and raised her glass. Her brown hair was long and swept back, her freshly-scrubbed porcelain skin fairly glowing in its purity. She wore a dramatically-cut aubergine dress that sat slightly off her shoulders. A grownup dress—an *adult* dress— adorned her body for the first time. She knew that she looked radiant and beautiful and powerful. She looked up and down the long table at the faces she didn't recognize, and then took a deep breath, remembering all she had learned about speaking in public.

"Good nobles, friends, and family members, the day of my adulthood has arrived. My parents, your king and queen, have taught me well. I am humbled by your presence, and I pledge to you that when my time comes, I will be as wise, as just, as strong of a leader as my parents before me. Now, let us eat, and let this feast be the harbinger of good tidings, of prosperity, and of the bright future we all can share!" With that she lifted the glass and drank.

When she lowered the cup, she noticed all the nobles staring at her, remaining stock-still. The queen cleared her throat and stood, applauding, and soon all the nobles joined in.

Dread washed over the princess. What had just happened? Her first speech to the nobles, short as it was, met with stony silence. She forced a smile onto her face, and choked down a few bites of the food.

After the feast, a band of musicians led by the blond-tressed lute player began to set up, and the nobles prepared to dance. But the king and queen drew their daughter aside, away from the crowd.

"My dear," the king began, "it was a wonderful speech."

"No one seemed to like it," the princess said.

"I'm afraid we've made some incorrect assumptions," the queen continued. "It was never our intention to burden you with the leadership of the kingdom."

Rachel's jaw dropped open. "What? Then—why have I spent years learning science and mathematics? Potions and medicines? Literature and poetry?"

The king glanced sideways at his wife. "To win an appropriate suitor," he said. "A prince from a neighboring kingdom with whom we can share peace and prosperity."

Fury rose in Rachel's chest. "I—I'm to be sold off to a prince like a common whore?"

The queen's head snapped back as if slapped. "Certainly not! This is the highest honor!"

"The highest honor?" Rachel scoffed. "Why, I'm nothing but currency to you! I'm the coin you pay to another country!"

"Do not talk to your mother like that!"

Princess Rachel turned with a dramatic flick of her long skirts and stomped off.

She ignored the king and queen calling after her, and wanted to get away from everything—from the nobles she had tried to impress, from her parents' expectations. In fact, she wanted to leave behind her whole life as a princess.

She walked past the castle gardens and through the groves of fruit trees. She hadn't ever been this far from the castle before, but her quick pace and the fresh air made her feel more in control. She might have to succumb to an arranged marriage eventually, but she didn't have to like it.

She continued walking and cursing her parents under her breath. She didn't notice that the path became less even, the trees more dense. She didn't notice that the sunlight had more trouble filtering through the boughs here. She tripped over a tree root but caught herself before she fell.

She looked up—and didn't recognize anything. She looked back the way she came, but several possible routes through the trees faced her. Was it the path between the two birch trees, or the maple and the cedar? Or were either of them real trails?

Oh no.

She was in the Forest of Shadows.

Panic begin to rise in her chest—and then a loud rustling of underbrush sounded behind her.

Rachel spun around.

A sleek, stunning unicorn appeared between two majestic oaks. Its coat was a brilliant white, almost glowing. With rippling muscles along its side, powerful forelegs, and a silvery tail, the brilliant animal took Rachel's breath away.

It was the most beautiful creature the princess had ever seen.

The unicorn stared at the princess with deep brown eyes that Rachel felt boring into her soul. She'd looked radiant, beautiful, and powerful at the beginning of the feast, but how long had she been fleeing through the forest? Had brambles scratched her perfect porcelain skin? Had thistles caught her alluring aubergine dress?

Then the unicorn's stare deepened, and Rachel was

magnetically drawn to this shimmering horned stallion. She took a step forward, and then another. The unicorn shook its head—was that in surprise?—but continued locking eyes with the princess. Closer and closer, Rachel walked. When she stood no more than five feet from the magical beast, she reached out her hand to touch it. Her fingertips brushed the unicorn's face, just above the nose.

Boom.

Bolts of intense pleasure flooded the princess's body. Rachel's eyes clamped shut.

The shimmering vibrations started in her fingertips, where she was touching the unicorn, and the pleasure coursed through her arms, to her heart, then descended directly to her sex.

Rachel gasped.

She'd read about the emotions she was experiencing in those pilfered poems.

She'd studied the descriptions of the physical sensations in those forbidden anatomy chapters.

She'd perused the potion formulas and memorized the elixir recipes for curing heartache and for summoning lust. But none of the books had prepared her for this.

For the first time in her life, she felt the physical sensations and they were everything her parents had tried to protect her from—all the highs and lows of the world, all the ins and outs, and betweens and throughs.

She heard the moan that escaped her lips, then another and another.

Her whole body quivered with need.

This is why the Forest of Shadows is forbidden.

She couldn't control the sensations, and she couldn't stand the ache and the desire.

With Herculean effort, she pulled her fingertips off the unicorn's face. Rachel opened her eyes, gasping for breath, and looked the unicorn in the eyes.

His eyes had changed. The burning curiosity that drew her to him now was replaced by desire—the same desire that Rachel felt between her legs. She'd never felt passion so strongly, and she'd never seen it reflected in another's eyes. The intensity of her emotions thrilled her and frightened her and she stretched her hand out again.

The unicorn quickly turned and ran off into the forest.

"Wait!"

Rachel's call echoed through the trees, but the unicorn paid no heed. The princess stood for a moment, stunned.

And then she sprinted after him.

Princess Rachel ran as fast as she could, trying to keep up. His shimmering coat was in high contrast to the shadows of the forest, so she easily kept him in sight. Through the underbrush, between young saplings, over fallen logs, and around boulders, the princess pursued the majestic unicorn. She focused on the shining silvery tail, the glimmering coat, and the dappling sunlight glinting off the horn. She ran until her lungs were straining, and then ran some more.

But wait—how could she be keeping up?

The unicorn could run much faster than her. He was still ahead, but she was easily able to follow and never out of sight.

Maybe the unicorn is injured.

Then Rachel stopped dead in her tracks, a chill running down her spine.

The unicorn wasn't injured. It was *luring* her into the forest.

She might have been able to pick her way back before. But now? All the trees looked the same. The underbrush that she had crashed through had melted together again. The vines hanging from the branches above her swung back and forth ominously. Her heart pounded in her ears. This is why the king and queen had forbidden her from entering the Forest of Shadows.

She looked up again, and the unicorn was gone. Had it run over the ridge? Did she really want to follow him anymore?

Then Rachel heard a loud rustling behind her, and she spun on her heels.

No one was there.

Then something grabbed both her wrists. She tried to spin again to no avail. She pulled and fought, dug her heels in. The vines had descended and wrapped around her wrists. She struggled, but the vines were strong and their grip was tight. They wrapped around her before she could kick them off. Another vine wrapped itself around her torso. Princess Rachel's eyes widened because no matter what she did, the magic vines had complete control over her. In the next second, the vines lifted her off the ground and she squealed in surprise. Floating above the ground, she spied the unicorn, his horn glowing.

She floated close enough to the unicorn that she could have touched him if her wrists hadn't been bound. She locked eyes with the unicorn again. He was controlling the vines somehow, she was sure of it, but his eyes were full of the same intense desire she'd seen in the clearing.

Then the horn's glow spread throughout the unicorn's entire body. The princess couldn't tear her eyes away from the golden glow, and he began to transform.

The unicorn's long face shrank into itself, his forelegs twisting, changing their angle to the rest of the torso. The beast reared up on its hindlegs and lost its bright white hair, its unshod hooves uncurling into hands. The mandible of the unicorn shortened into a strong jawline, its belly changing into a well-defined chest with hard abdominal muscles, and its legs thickening with sinewy thigh and calf muscles. Transforming, but not shrinking, however, was the man-beast's phallus. It darkened from the heady white of the unicorn to a deep brown color—clearly matching the beautiful, perfect skin of the man the unicorn became. The phallus was erect and thick, much thicker than the illustrations in the anatomy book.

She couldn't take her eyes off it.

She remembered some of the language of the love poems, some of the vulgarities that made her feel funny inside. *Cock. Manhood. Sheath. Penetrating. Seed.*

Sin.

As he completed his transformation, he spread his arms wide, palms out, as if conducting the vines that held her. She raised her gaze from his impossibly hard erection to his beautiful human face for the first time, his wide nose and softly jutting cheekbones a powerful contrast with his smooth, glowing skin and gently-shut eyes.

Princess Rachel strained against her bonds. She had to get closer and touch him again. Would the pleasure flood her as it had when he was a unicorn? She moaned and mewled.

She hoped the desire in her eyes was as obvious as the desire in his.

He opened his eyes and stared directly into hers.

She gasped, a shock of lightning passed between them, as the rest of the world sprang into darkness.

The two of them, locked in synchronicity.

The cosmos whirled around her, the sounds of wind and rain and thunder exploding around her, and yet echoing like a distant memory.

"There is a great danger within you," the beautiful man murmured.

"I—I don't understand," Rachel said.

"I am Prince Jalen of the Shadows," he said, "and no human has ever affected me like this before."

"Please," Princess Rachel moaned, "please, do anything you want to me. Ravish me, use me, anything." She leaned forward and stretched to try to touch him.

"Did you not feel the power of your touch in the clearing?" Prince Jalen asked sharply.

"I—I did feel it," Rachel admitted. "I want to feel it again. I want to touch you. I want you to touch me. Please."

At that moment, the vine holding her right wrist released its grip, and Princess Rachel pulled her hand free, immediately placing it on Prince Jalen's powerful chest, the pectoral muscle flinching under her fingers.

A tingle began in Rachel's hand, different than touching the unicorn's snout, but it intensified, moving throughout her body. It felt as if warm honey flowed everywhere in her veins, the delicious feeling strongest between her legs.

"Oh—" Prince Jalen said, and his erection jolted and bobbed. "I—I cannot understand how a lowly human can make me feel this way." He looked at her and pressed his lips together, trying to regain control. "Who *are* you?"

"I am Princess Rachel," she said, sliding her hand down and lightly touching his shaft.

Prince Jalen drew in a sharp breath. "No—it cannot be. You're the princess? From the castle?"

"I am."

"The prophecy," Prince Jalen murmured. "I must fight it."

"I don't want you to fight it," Rachel said. "I want it. I want *you*."

"But—war with the humans—"

"Please," Rachel whispered. "You—you make me feel things I never knew before."

"You too, my princess."

"Anything you want," Rachel said, stronger this time.

Prince Jalen stepped forward and they kissed.

The poems and the textbooks had nothing on the kiss. She let Jalen take over, exploring her mouth with his tongue, his hands pulling her skirts up desperately. She was hot and wet between her legs, sensations she wasn't used to, but her prince's touch melted what little fear she had left until all she felt was passion and lust.

Prince Jalen's hard cock, still in Rachel's hand, touched her stomach as he tore off her undergarments.

"Yes," Rachel moaned, "yes, Jalen, yes." She stroked him back and forth, trying to remember what the poems and texts had said about male stimulation.

Then he hesitated.

"We cannot anger the universe like this, my sweet princess."

"I don't care. Fill me, Jalen. Fill me with your manhood.

Make me your bride." She continued to stroke him, his cock getting thicker and harder still.

Drawing a deep breath, Jalen gently took her face in his hands. "Oh, my beautiful princess," he said, "you don't even know why this is so wrong. And you have no idea what we need to do to make the world right afterward."

She shifted her hips and positioned his cock at her entrance. "It feels like the world is right to me."

"I'm not strong enough to resist," Jalen murmured.

He thrust himself inside of her as she released him from her grip, and the world spun.

Like a bolt of lightning, a flash flew through her mind. Her head filled with knowledge and techniques and capabilities—all of pleasuring Jalen. Like a roll of thread unspooling in the hard light of day, she saw exactly where to touch him, how to use her fingers, her nails, her tongue, her mouth. How to capture his manhood with her lips and buck her hips when he was inside her. She leaned forward and they kissed again, and she changed the angle of her pelvis and Jalen's breath caught.

"Oh—oh—my princess...."

"The universe must want this," Rachel groaned. "I—I don't know how I—"

Then sparks began in her stomach and intensified all the way down to her sex.

"How can you—" Jalen murmured between gasps.

Then the pleasure overcame her.

She didn't know how long it went on for, and she couldn't hear herself over the pounding in her veins and the buzzing of her clitoris. He quickened his thrusting, just a little, and the sensations cranked up again. She must have been moaning and screaming and groaning his name. She wanted to touch him everywhere, run her hands all over his beautiful chest and stomach and shoulders and arms and face. She felt his hands on her breasts—when had her dress come off?— and then she felt him give a burst of hard thrusts as he filled her up with his seed, as the love poem said, and the crescendo of her pleasure peaked and slowly, wonderfully, slid down.

The sky split open with a loud crack of thunder.

"What have we done?" Prince Jalen moaned.

Rachel traced her thumb from his cheek to his lips. "I'm not sure I care, my love."

As I go over that section of the story tonight, as soon as I read the part of Prince Jalen and Princess Rachel coming together to touch their lips for the first time, I rotate my hips in my seat. Oh wow, I'm randy and ready for Jalen, and there's still a few more hours before he gets here.

I lift my ass off the leather chair and slip my sweatpants and my panties down to my ankles. I edit a couple of typos —I misspelled both 'tongue' and 'mouth' when describing their kiss. I save my work, and then I give into the needs of my body. I think about Jalen's torso, the firmness of his chest, and his solid stomach muscles under his soft skin. I breathe in as I put my left hand between my legs, and I can *smell* him. His leathery cologne is his signature, and I inhale fully. The thought of him with me, holding me with the magic vines around my wrists, gives way to an immense pleasure immediately ramrodding through me.

I'm still holding my right hand over the keyboard, trying to fool myself into believing I'd be able to continue *concentrating* on the story, much less type it with one hand, but I keep my hand poised above the letters as I increase my fingers' urgency. The words on the monitor blur, and I moan. He wants to obey the rules of the Forest of Shadows, but he's so driven by the animal need for Princess Rachel, he can't stop touching her. I want to keep my eyes open and keep reading this unicorn-and-princess sex scene, but I give in, closing my eyes.

The real Jalen appears before me in my vision, holding my wrists firmly against the arms of the chair, the molded plastic pressing against the flesh, but not too hard. He whispers in my ear.

"I want to ravish your beautiful body, my princess." His breath is warm, yet I get a shiver down my spine. "I want to see your legs shake when you come. I want to fill up your sweet pussy with my seed."

I gasp and open my eyes. Jalen disappears. "Fuck it," I say out loud, and stand up. I kick off the sweats and my underwear, and hurry, bottomless, into our bedroom, where I throw off the comforter and climb on the bed. I get on my knees and stick my ass up in the air, fantasizing that Jalen would take me from behind—unicorn-style. *Hah.*

I go back to being Princess Rachel, putting my arms above my head, with my wrists next to the headboard, imagining them held firm by the vines. I imagine Jalen positioned behind me with his big cock at my sweet entrance. His large hands hold me firmly by my hips, and I squeak with need, fantasizing about Jalen's impossibly hard, thick cock plunging into my sex over and over again.

"Fuck, Jalen," I groan, "I can't believe how you just threw me down on the bed, my big ass in the air, just to have your way with me."

"I don't ever want to be away from you again," I picture Jalen saying. I put my left hand on my ass cheek and give it a brief slap. "Oh yeah," my fantasy Jalen says, "you like it when I smack your sweet ass, don't you?"

"Oh yes, Jalen," I moan, putting my right hand between my legs and playing with my clit, "smack my ass harder." I give it a firmer slap. "Fuck me like you own me. Like I'm your dirty princess who you'll keep captive forever—" and then my orgasm hits hard. My legs won't hold my weight any more. I roll onto my side, my fingers still between my legs, shoved inside myself, as I feel my muscles clench again and again.

I gasp for air, Jalen's hot breath still a memory in my ear, the fantasy still alive of his cock tightening, pulsing, as wave after wave of his hot, delicious cum shoots into my eager pussy.

For a moment all I can do is feel the pulsing, the rhythm, the heat of our two bodies, and then it fades into silence, only a faint ringing and the sound of my harsh, stilted breathing as I come down from the high.

I take a deep, shuddering breath and then expel it in a rush. My heart beats more slowly, closer to normal, and I open my eyes.

I'm in the bed I share with my beautiful husband. My mouth is sticky from being dry, and I'm naked except for my T-shirt. I gingerly open my legs, feeling the slight stickiness of my juices. I smile wistfully.

Carefully, I slide to the edge of the bed and then swing

my feet to the floor. I stand up, not using my right hand and still keeping it from dripping onto the sheets or the carpet. I pad to the bathroom, turn on the sink, and wash my hands.

I pull the T-shirt down, walk downstairs, and turn all the lights off except for the floor lamp at the entry from the garage. I make sure the door is deadbolted and the porch-light is lit, so Jalen won't be coming home in the dark, and then climb the stairs again. I close my story because I don't want Jalen stumbling across this when he comes home. It's difficult enough connecting with him with his travel sched-ule. I don't need to have a conversation about why I'm writing smutty stories with him turning into a unicorn.

I turn out the light in the office, and then, heavy-limbed and heavy-lidded, I stumble back into our bedroom and get into bed, thinking about the night I just spent reading my dirty story and getting off.

I feel naughty, like I'd done something secret and wrong, but I kind of like the feeling. I pull the covers over me, dressed just in the T-shirt, nothing on the bottom. I wonder if I should put panties on, but I'm too tired to get out of bed.

Laying back, I feel the sheets against my bare skin. I haven't slept without panties since the early days of marriage. Jalen and I would sleep naked together all the time *before* we were married. Before we were even officially dating.

Jalen would *love* to come home and crawl into bed and find his wife naked, just like old times. I sit up in the dark-ness and pull the T-shirt over my head, throwing it on the floor. I turn onto my side, tug the covers back up, and feel the unfamiliar sensation of the sheets sliding over me.

I picture Jalen in bed with me, wrapping his powerful

arms around me from behind and pulling me into his body, his cock hard against the uncovered small of my back. I shiver, not from cold, but from my body's hunger. I'm still not satiated. Reading my fantasy unleashes a beast in me just as powerful as the unicorn.

As I debate about whether I have the energy to stay up until Jalen gets home, I fall asleep.

THE NEW BOSS

I wake up with gray light filtering through the window, and I roll over. I'm still naked, but Jalen isn't next to me. His side of the bed doesn't even look slept in. I blink, and in spite of the light, I wonder if it's still nighttime. But no, the clock on my bedside table reads 6:23.

Dammit. I wanted Jalen to find me in bed last night, horny and naked, but he didn't even make it home.

Suddenly, panic hits me. His plane was supposed to land late at night, and he was supposed to make the two-hour drive home. What if he got into a car accident, or what if his plane crashed?

I reach for the phone on my bedside table, but it's not there. Oh, that's right—I left it in the office, while I was reading through the book last night. I grab my robe from the closet, put it on, and then I run into the office.

The phone screen shows a text from Jalen.

Too tired to drive home

Going to a cheap hotel – should be home by 10 tomorrow
morning

Whew. That's a relief. I sit down, my heart pounding, and take deep breaths to calm myself.

I hear my alarm go off in our bedroom—it's 6:25, the time I normally wake up to go to work. I sigh. Another sexless night for me. It's been way too long. I text Jalen back.

Have a safe drive home
Thanks for letting me know you stayed in SF
I'm so horny for you please let me fuck your brains out when
I get home tonight

No, I don't really send that last text. In fact, I didn't even type out the whole thing before I deleted it completely.

I walk into our master bathroom to shower and get ready for the day.

꧁꧂

Traffic is thankfully light and I make it to work early. The morning passes in a caffeine-fueled haze. I walk a couple of blocks to Chando's Tacos for lunch, getting three of their carne asada street tacos, and sit at the counter with my Diet Coke waiting for my order. I pull up the *Sacramento Bee*'s app on my phone and browse the day's headlines. One catches my eye.

Swiss Firm Sells Woodward Reynolds Division to Beckett for $2B

Beckett. The famous Sacramento financial firm that brokered the Q-Merit deal. The firm were Alicia Parker— sorry, Alicia *Hawthorne*—works now.

No wonder she said she would see me sooner than I thought. I groan.

I hope Jalen doesn't have to work anywhere near her. They're both in sales, of course, so I'm sure they'll be assigned to different customers. And I hope the fact that Beckett is local means Jalen's travel will be minimal. Sure, maybe he'll have to go to a few clients, but maybe they won't be in London or Lucerne.

A queasy feeling nestles in the pit of my stomach, though, and the cook has to call "Order for Rachel! Three carne asada!" before I snap myself out of it and move. Something about this really doesn't feel right.

I grab the basket of tacos and go back to my stool, where I read the article. The article never mentions Alicia Hawthorne. I wasn't really expecting it to, but it wouldn't have surprised me. They only mention the CEO of Beckett Financial, and he just spews the same platitudes that I've seen after every acquisition.

When I call Jalen but it goes to voicemail. I wonder if they made him come in today, after spending the night in a cheap airport hotel and driving over a hundred miles home.

When I get back to the office, I need to prepare for a meeting with the bridge construction team, but I'm distracted. My eyes glaze over as I read their report on the type of concrete they've planned to use, as well as the material handling costs. I really don't feel like double-checking their math, but I see one of my colleagues questioned why they weren't choosing a cheaper, stronger alternative. That's at least one thing I can bring up in the meeting.

I open my browser and type the URL for CareerChain, and enter the name *Alicia Hawthorne*. There are several hits, but the photo of the former Alicia Parker shows the woman I'm searching for.

Her background is impressive. She's been with Beckett for almost six years. Crazy that she's lived in Sacramento longer than Jalen and I have. She started on a low rung at Beckett, as an associate advisor, but she's moved up in the company quickly, rarely staying in a role more than eighteen months.

Oh, and she's got a new role. Starting date of yesterday.

International Finance Group Director.

Oh no.

That's the title of Jalen's boss, or rather, his *former* boss.

My stomach clenches. Jalen will be reporting to his ex-girlfriend. The one who still carries a torch for him. The one who hates me.

§◆

I rally after lunch, take charge of the meeting, and guide the team through the disagreement in concrete specifications. I review some sections of documentation and close out a couple of sections on the project plan. The bridge is still years away from completion, but the groundbreaking moves closer than it was this morning.

The productivity high wears off on the drive home, and

the specter of Alicia Hawthorne looms in my brain. I pull into our driveway, but it seems I beat Jalen home. As I walk in the front door, my phone buzzes. It's a text from Jalen.

You won't believe who my new boss is

I shake my head and we start to text back and forth.

Rachel: Alicia Parker?
Jalen: Yes. How did you know?
Rachel: Long story
Jalen: I'm supposed to have a strategy meeting over dinner
*   with her tonight*
Jalen: Sorry – I know I just got home but I don't see how I
*   can say no*

I have half a mind to show up at their getting-to-know-you dinner wearing that red sweater from high school that I know shows off my tits. Man, Alicia would *really* hate that. Too bad I don't have the sweater anymore.

I text him back.

So how worried do I need to be that you're having dinner
*   with your ex-girlfriend?*

Almost immediately, three bouncing dots appear, indicating that he's typing something in response. Then they disappear. They reappear. They disappear again.

Jalen: Worried about my job security? I don't know.
Rachel: And what about other stuff?

Jalen: Oh, hell no
Jalen: But honestly I'm not sure about reporting to Alicia
Jalen: She's already made some weird comments

I sigh. Of course. And my curiosity can't be contained.

Rachel: Like what? Anything written down?
Jalen: Little stuff – and nothing in email or texts, only stuff
she said to me
Jalen: Saying I look as good as I did in high school
Jalen: Might be innocent but it feels weird

Hmph. So, really, about what I had to go through with one of my male bosses at the startup every day for the year I reported to him. Little stuff. "Wow, Rachel, that dress is very *flattering* on you." Asking me to go grab the presentation off his desk during a meeting, and feeling his eyes on my ass as I leave the room. I text him back, but I know the answer.

Can you go to HR

His response is almost immediate.

Are you kidding?
A black man accusing a white woman of harassment
During my first week at this new company?

Of course, he's got a point. Even if the situation sucks, I'm glad Jalen is telling me. His honesty about the best I can hope for, under the circumstances. If things get strange at work, Jalen can request to be transferred, even if it doesn't look good to his new management. Plus Alicia has never stayed in any position at Beckett very long. Even if it's a nightmare, maybe it'll only be a nightmare for a few months before she's promoted out of there. Also, her husband talked about Jalen in the coffee shop, which means she's told her husband all about Jalen, too. If it's as awkward for him as it is for me, he might not *want* Jalen reporting to her. I type out another text.

Did you say anything to her

This time, there's no response. Maybe he had to go into a meeting, or maybe he's driving in the car, or maybe he's already at the restaurant with her.

No, that's bullshit. She *has* said something to him. Something that's made him uncomfortable.

And then a little voice inside my head piped up.

You and Jalen haven't had sex in a couple of months.

Shut up, little voice.

It's true. It might not be anything you did, but he's now with his ex, someone who knows the world of international finance a lot better than you. You know Alicia is smarter than to just bring up her attraction to Jalen in front of him. She'll be subtle. She'll flirt so mildly that Jalen won't know why he feels uncomfortable. She didn't have anything in common with him in high school, but now she does. The mystique of the Amsterdam stock exchange is something she and Jalen can talk about for hours. You know he'd be nodding off in five minutes if you start talking about concrete curing strength curves.

Those sure aren't the curves he's interested in. I smirk.

Yeah, good point.

Alicia might be his ex-girlfriend, and she may still look

terrific, but I have to remember that even though *I* may not like my body, Jalen does. My curvy, sensual body turned his head senior year in high school, all those years ago. He's the one who broke up with Alicia. He's the one who asked me out. And I'm the one who said yes.

THE FIRST DATE

*N*ews of my date with senior stud Jalen spread like a tsunami over the school. I started hearing that we had both been madly attracted to each other for months, but Alicia Parker had gotten in the way. The rumors varied widely in detail. First I heard that I had blackmailed him into dumping Alicia, then I heard that Alicia had black-mailed Jalen into dating her in the first place, and then I heard that Jalen had been trying to get a threesome going with the two of us for weeks.

He must have heard the rumors, too, because when we passed each other in the hall in the days before our date he smiled but his eyes revealed a wariness. News got back to me that he found out I was a virgin. Later that day I heard Alicia Parker was slut-shaming me by telling people I'd fucked nerdy guys from the Chess Club or the Math Olympics Team. (Not that I wouldn't have. A couple of those guys were actually really cute.)

The rumors got wilder as the week went on. On Wednesday at lunch a freshman asked me if it was true that

I'd been gangbanged by the boys' badminton team. I tried for a few seconds to come up with a clever play on words with "shuttlecock" but my brain failed me, and the freshman ran off, tittering.

Between fifth and sixth period, when I was counting down the days until the end of the week and my date with Jalen, Alicia Parker passed me in the hall and knocked the books out of my arms. She fake coughed "whore" as I bent down to pick them up.

Elaine, who had been walking next to me, shouted after her, "You're just jealous because Jalen can't get enough of Rachel's fucking gorgeous tits, and you're flat as a board." The whole hallway erupted in laughter, although I couldn't tell if it was at me or at Alicia, or just in general at Elaine's ridiculous statement.

After school, Elaine's comment was all over campus, and I noticed Jalen's friends giving me more appreciative looks as they passed, which was a little on the creepy side. As I turned the corner toward my locker ten minutes after the last bell, I heard one of his friends call Alicia by the nickname "Board," which I assumed was a reference to Elaine's insult of *flat-as-a*.

She wasn't, of course. I'd actually been jealous of Alicia's breasts, nicely shaped but manageable. I had to be constantly aware of where my breasts were, and how much they were making themselves known, whether it was visible cleavage in a V-neck shirt, jutting out too far in a tight sweater, or jiggling too much in a tank top. But my envy of Alicia's breasts made no difference to her. The look on her face showed me that the nickname bothered her.

Over the rest of that week before our date, after Elaine

had pointed out that Jalen was less than suave when admiring my body, I started to notice every time Jalen glanced at me. I hadn't really noticed how much attention he'd ever given me.

Honestly, even after Elaine told me that Jalen had had a crush on me, or at least a crush on my curves, I could hardly believe it. I mean, this was *the* guy in school. I was supposed to be a weirdo.

Finally, Friday night arrived. I called Elaine a few times after school, and I finally settled on the infamous red sweater and a black skirt that ended just above my knees. The red sweater was thin and clung to my curves, and I was worried that it would look too lascivious. I appraised myself in the mirror, and finally decided that it was secret-sexy. Perfect for a first date with the most sought-after boy in my class when I still lived at home with my parents. I wore low black heels as well, which might have been a little too dressy for a dinner-and-a-movie date, but I figured I'd rather be a little more dressed up than too casual.

When he came to pick me up from my house, he handed me a small but tasteful bouquet of mums and purple daisies. I had fretted and stressed about my outfit. I'd wanted something sexy enough for him to appreciate the, *uh*, things he appreciated about me. I'd also wanted something that wasn't too much for him, either. Nothing that would invite the worst sex clown urges. Besides, he might have thought it a joke, and I didn't want to be shown up while wearing a neckline that plunged to my navel.

Jalen smiled as he gave me the bouquet. "Wow, you look beautiful, Rachel."

"Thanks, Jalen." I gave him a once-over too. He wore

dark jeans, nice brown suede shoes, and a bright, crisp white long-sleeved dress shirt, popping against his complexion. Somehow the shirt both covered his upper body and accentuated it, making his shoulders look broader. The top two buttons were undone at his neck, but the gap didn't look too low or cheesy, as his thick neck and wide chest took up most of the visual space. He didn't wear a necklace, but the very edges of his collarbones were visible next to his collar. I found myself staring at the edges of his collarbones with the same hunger I'd had staring at his ass the day he asked me out.

Damn. *Every* part of him was phenomenal. Standing in the hall, holding the bouquet, I wanted to rip his clothes off and do *things* to him. Things I'd only read about. Things that would really make my father uncomfortable if he could read my mind.

"I'll, uh, go find a vase," I said, as my father strode down the hallway toward us.

I went to the kitchen to put the flowers in water, and when I came back, Jalen was shaking hands with my father, looking him in the eye. My father was glancing at him warily, and I couldn't figure out my emotions. I wanted to have my guard up in case this was still a joke. But every look Jalen gave me, every half smile, every brush of his hand against mine—it all was real. Elaine's stories of Jalen crushing on me were true.

I smiled at my father and promised him I'd be home by midnight, and we left.

Our nervousness was heavy between us as we walked down the driveway to Jalen's Honda Accord, parked at the curb.

Most guys in the Aycees crowd, especially the ones on the football team, had sports cars, or brand-new four-wheel-drive pickups. (Sometimes with the fake testicles hanging off the trailer hitch, which was gross. But those guys got laid anyway.) Jalen didn't seem embarrassed by his practical Japanese sedan, however, and I noticed it was shiny and spotless. He must have washed it.

He opened the door of the car for me. The inside was incredibly clean. The black dashboard was even shiny, the way the interior looked in my mom's car after a professional detail.

That's when the truth of the evening hit me with certainty. Yes, Elaine had said it, and yes, I'd seen it in his eyes, but the shiny dashboard was proof that this was a real date, and not only that, but he was *into* me.

That realization might have calmed me down, but no. I was actually more nervous than I'd been before. I actually had a *chance* with Jalen Jefferson. No one but the top echelon of girls at Montrose High got a chance with him. And I had jumped the line, punched above my class, outkicked my coverage, all those mildly humorous sports metaphors I heard for ugly guys dating hot girls. Here I was, the purple-haired, size-12, journalism geek, on a date with the hottest boy in school.

My mouth went dry.

I forced myself to smile at Jalen as he got in the car and started it up. He fiddled with the stereo and the sound of the CD changer started and stopped, and then "Make Me Love You" came on, the volume perfect.

"I guess you've done your homework," I said.

"My homework? Like, for class?"

"No, silly. Your homework on my favorite band. The Tiger Lily Serenade. I didn't think anyone else had even heard of them."

Jalen smiled sheepishly. "Yeah, well, I guess I did ask your friend what music you liked. But I swear, I already had this CD."

I looked at him out of the corner of my eye. "Impossible. No one has this CD. I found it in an indie store near A-State last year."

A smile turned up the corner of his lips. "On Fifth Street, right? Permanent Records?"

"Yeah," I said, impressed. "It's nice to know the hipsters have a purpose in life. Keeping indie record stores in business."

Jalen laughed easily, his beautiful eyes squinting. I smiled in return, watching his face closely.

Aw, shit, girl, that's a real laugh. And your joke wasn't even that funny. Jalen Jefferson's got it bad for you.

He reached to the ignition and turned the key again. It made a horrible, high-pitched grinding noise and Jalen let go of the key as if he'd been shocked.

"Car's already on," I said, before I could stop myself.

He nodded, not looking at me, and he put the car into gear and drove to the restaurant.

Jalen had made reservations at Arturo's, a popular Italian spot down the street from a neighboring high school. He and I had been quiet in the car and were equally quiet as we waited for a seat.

"So," I said, clearing my throat, "who do you have for Government?"

We made small talk about school for a few minutes. We

didn't share any classes, but we had the same teacher for British Lit.

Jalen was quiet for a moment and then turned to me. "Hey, can I ask you a question?"

"Uh, sure." My stomach had butterflies.

"I hear we get called the 'Aycees' all the time. Do you know why?"

I chuckle. "Sure. It's because you're the cool kids. And AC stands for air conditioning."

Jalen leaned back in his seat. "Seriously? That's it?"

"Kind of obvious, I know."

He shook his head, laughing. "We thought it was supposed to be an insult, but we couldn't figure out what it was supposed to mean."

"What else could 'Aycee' possibly mean?"

"Alternating current, for one thing."

"Yeah, you guys all have electric personalities."

"Or like infected with something. Like the last AC in celiac or hemophiliac."

I grin. "Or Cadillac. Or Balzac."

Jalen's eyes widen. "Or *what?* Ball sack?"

I feel the color rise to my face. "Oh my God, no. A French writer. Honoré de Balzac. He wrote *The Human Comedy.*" I laugh nervously. "I wasn't planning to mention your testicles until *after* dinner."

It's out of my mouth before I can stop it.

Jalen smirks. "Good. I didn't want to be the first one to bring them up."

I want to crawl under a rock and die.

The maître-d' seated us after a couple of minutes, and we were led to a small two-person table pretty much in the center of the restaurant. I felt like everyone was staring at me; who *was* this girl who had the gall to show up with the hottest guy in the whole town, if not the greater Phoenix metropolitan area?

When we were seated across from each other, I looked around. No one was paying any attention to us. I took a deep breath, less smoothly than I had hoped, and breathed out. I opened the menu and stared at everything. I didn't want to eat anything with a red sauce that might stain, but I didn't really like the heavy cream sauces. I turned the page from the pastas to the entrees. Maybe a chicken dish? Maybe salmon? No, nothing to give me fish breath. I looked up at Jalen. He was looking at the menu with just as much panic in his eyes as I was sure I had in mine.

I couldn't concentrate, and I flipped back to the pasta page.

The server, a pretty Asian woman probably in her early twenties, was surprisingly attentive. At first it was nice, especially considering that a high school kid on his first date might not be financially solvent enough to tip very well. But after she took our order, she put her hand on his menu and purposely ran her fingers down the back of his hand. He flinched and dropped the menu onto the table.

"My apologies, sir," she said.

He narrowed his eyes. "No problem."

She was more subtle for about twenty minutes after that, although she came around a lot to fill up his soda and my water glass. When she cleared our appetizer plates, she fired another big salvo. She dropped a fork on the floor, and bent over at the waist to pick it up, her butt firm and round in her tight black pants, aimed so that Jalen would notice.

Jalen didn't even turn his head toward the server's ass. Instead, he leaned forward, elbows on the table, toward me. In a low voice he said—not so that the whole restaurant could hear, but so that I could, and she could, "Did I tell you how beautiful you look tonight?"

He had, but it was nice to hear the compliment again.

That's how the whole dinner went. Jalen and I were both nervous and awkward and weird around each other. For me, the stakes were so high once Elaine told me that Jalen actually liked me that I overthought everything. I froze up. I didn't know what was going through Jalen's mind. Maybe he expected me to throw myself at him, but then when he got me out on the date he saw me in a different light. Perhaps he wasn't as attracted to me as he'd led me to believe.

Or maybe he'd believed the false rumors from Alicia Parker that I'd wrap my tits around his dick on the first date.

False rumors? Who am I kidding? He was so good-looking that all he'd have to do was ask. I wouldn't have known what I was doing, but the way he'd been looking at me, I got the distinct impression that I wouldn't have needed to do much of the work.

I was too distracted during the Tarantino film to enjoy most of it. There were a few great lines of dialogue, but I was thinking of how I could rescue the evening, and I wasn't following the plot. By the time the climactic scene came around, the one where most of the main characters die in a shootout, I was no longer concentrating on the movie. I was trying to plan what I would do on the drive home. How would we say goodnight? How could I get him to kiss me?

He was a perfect gentleman again, holding the passenger door open for me, putting my favorite band's

CD on again. He asked if I wanted to stop for ice cream, and I, feeling full from the smoked chicken pappardelle, declined. I tried not to make a big deal out of not wanting dessert, and I wondered how I could make it clear that I had really enjoyed myself without seeming like a complete idiot.

Then, way too soon, we were in front of my house. The clock on the dashboard read 10:18 PM. We were still an hour and forty-five minutes from my curfew.

I looked at Jalen, biting my lip. "I had a really nice time," I said, even though I'd been tongue-tied and self-conscious the whole date. "Do you, uh, want to walk me up?"

He paused for a minute and then smiled. It wasn't the easy smile he had earlier when he laughed at my joke. I couldn't get a good read on him, but I felt uneasiness wash over me. I was about to lose out on a second date if I didn't do something soon.

He got out of the car and opened my door a second later. We walked up the driveway, still in the awkward silence. I debated reaching out and taking his hand, but that didn't feel right.

Say something, Rachel. Anything. Let him know that you weren't yourself tonight.

My nerves were all over the place, and I could barely think above the hum of my intense physical craving for him. I looked at his face, so handsome it was as if it was sculpted. I wanted to lick him all over. I wanted him to show me the way he liked to have his dick sucked. I opened my mouth.

"It's after dinner," I said. "We could discuss your ball sack now."

He laughed, and I was mortified, but I managed to turn

my shock at what I'd just said into what I hoped was a cute giggle.

"I had a nice evening," he said, a few steps from the door. "Tarantino's great. Kind of a weird film, but I bet I'll wake up tomorrow appreciating it more."

"Me too," I squeaked, turning toward him and hoping, wishing, even begging for a kiss. I started to open my mouth to say all the stuff my inner self was screaming. He could fuck me in the backseat right now. All he'd have to do was ask.

He took me into his arms, and I hoped he'd ravish me with his mouth, but no. It was a hug. I embraced him in return, cursing my body for being so stiff and uninviting. Even so, being that close to him was wonderful. I pushed my boobs into him, hoping to excite him enough to go a little further with our physical affection.

Alas, it wasn't to be. He broke from the embrace. "Have a great night," he said. "I'll see you at school on Monday." He gave me a little half wave as he turned, walking toward his Accord, his keys in his hand.

I took my house key out of my purse and unlocked the door. There was a reading light on in the living room. It was my dad. "Hey, punkin," he said. "How was your date?"

"It was all right," I said.

He looked up at me, a look of concern masked poorly by false disinterest. "Only all right?"

"Yeah. I mean, he's super-popular, and he's nice and everything, but, uh, I don't know how much we have in common."

Dad started to speak and then closed his mouth, then

opened it again. "It's, uh—well, this is kind of hard for me to say...."

"Just spit it out, Dad."

"It's—it's not because you think your mother and I have a problem with him, is it?"

I shook my head. "No, of course not."

"Because we don't. In fact, he's one of the good ones. Knows how to speak to adults. Doesn't just honk his horn and expect you to come running out."

"I know. I—I don't know why we didn't connect."

Really, it's because I can't get out of my own way. He and I should be up at the summit at South Mountain making out. Or in the backseat of his car, parked out by Lake Tempe, with him pulling the hem of my skirt up, my panties down around my knees, and him pumping his huge cock in and out of my needy, wet sex until we both come, hot, hard, breathing heavy, his penis throbbing, pulsating its sticky seed all over me as he whispers in my ear that he can't get close enough.

I was overcome with the urge to go into my room, strip, get into bed, and play with my clit and my pussy, fantasizing about Jalen Jefferson fucking me in every position imaginable, and even some I couldn't imagine.

I closed my eyes for just a second and pictured Jalen sucking my big hard nipples, his index and middle fingers dancing just above my clit, his cock thrusting into my pussy, over and over, until I lost control of myself, giving into my orgasm, my legs shaking and convulsing on their own, my vocalizations low and guttural.

"Are you okay?"

I opened my eyes and looked at my father. My face felt

hot and my mouth was parched. "I'm just tired. I guess I'll go to bed."

"Sorry your date wasn't better."

I shrugged and turned to leave the room. "It's okay. I'm sure there will be other guys."

"Yeah," Dad said. Then under his breath, "That's what I'm afraid of."

I walked down the hall to my room and closed the door behind me.

The walls of my room held a poster of The Tiger Lily Serenade, four people of vaguely indeterminate gender, two Asian, one white, and one black, staring at the camera with neutral faces, while behind them, a stark concrete and brick building was in the midst of collapsing. I walked around my bed to my stereo and put their latest CD in and then hit play. The driving beat and ephemeral sounds mixed together in the room, and I close my eyes, picturing myself in Jalen's car. I slipped off the low heels, stepping out of them with my eyes still closed. I pulled the tight red sweater over my head, and then I unzipped my skirt and kicked it off after it fell to my ankles.

After I turned off the overhead light, I got into bed with the music still on, just wearing my panties and bra, and pulled the covers up. My right hand pinched my nipple through the bra and then snaked down my belly and slipped underneath the waistband of my panties. I tentatively touched the skin just above my clit and then I bit my lip.

I fucked up my date with Jalen.

Instead of making out with him, instead of losing my virginity to him in the back seat of his Accord, instead of him giving me an orgasm better than my vibrator, he dropped me off an hour and forty-five minutes early.

I'd never been so horny for anyone in my life, though, and if I had messed up the date, I wondered if I could at least *pretend* that I hadn't. Pretend that he couldn't get enough of me. Pretend that he was desperate to get my clothes off, to see my naked curves the way he had only dreamed of when he'd stared at me in the hallways at school.

Arching my back, I reached behind myself to unhook my bra and then took the straps down from my shoulders and shucked the bra off, letting it fall onto the floor. I brought my knees up and pushed my panties from my waist to my calves, slipping them farther down to my ankles.

I was naked under the covers. I touched the folds of my labia. I was already wet. I brought my right hand to my mouth and sucked on my first two fingers. I pretended that they were Jalen's thick, strong fingers, and I sucked on them, using my tongue between the two digits, getting them sloppy, soaked in my own spit. Then I released my fingers from my mouth and brought them quickly to my sex. A string of spit hung between my mouth and my fingers for a split second before landing on my skin, a perfectly straight line from my pussy to my belly button, running between my breasts to my lower lip. Then I plunged the two fingers inside myself, my left hand pinching my nipple, fantasizing that it was Jalen taking me between his lips.

The song changed to "Make Me Love You," and it was all I could do not to melt into the bed. I fantasized about Jalen's hot breath in my ear, telling me how much he loved my curves. I moaned and then caught myself, not wanting to wake up my mother or my younger sister. The stereo was on, the music filling up the room, and it would probably cover up the sounds of my groaning, even if I was fantasizing about losing my virginity to the most beautiful senior at Montrose High. But I tried to be quiet anyway.

Another wicked thought flashed through my mind. If the stereo would cover the sounds of my moans, it would probably also cover the sounds of that vibrator I'd bought at the shop on Corning Avenue.

I propped myself up on one elbow and turned the bedside light on. I'd hidden it in the center drawer of my nightstand, which was sort of a catchall drawer that my mom despised because it was so messy... which made it a perfect hiding place. I had a lint-free cloth I'd bought just for the vibrator, a navy blue rectangle of fabric that looked clinical, and not at all like a sex-toy cleaning cloth, and certainly not a hiding place for a vibrator.

The vibrator was about eight inches long and had a short half U-shape about two-thirds of the way down. It wasn't a cheap model. It wasn't the most expensive one they'd had, either, but it was a solid investment. The woman at the adult store broke pretty much every preconceived notion I'd had of places like that.

First of all, I'd had the idea that all the employees at those places were creepy old dudes with four teeth and no social skills. The pretty goth girl behind the counter who complimented my hair was an unexpected plus. I thought I'd be intimidated with all the choices, which I was, but the girl behind the counter made me feel less embarrassed about asking my questions. After the first question or two, she said, "Oh, you're a *virgin*," and I blushed. Then she said, "Don't worry about it. It's good to explore your body so you can ask for what you want. You should enjoy your first time and unless you figure out the things you like, you won't be able to do anything to guide him. Or her," she added quickly. She asked me a couple more questions, asked me what my budget was. I had scrimped and saved for a few months, and had two hundred bucks earmarked for my purchase. Ten minutes later, I was the proud owner of a TwoFer O-Quest.

And now, I was fantasizing that the O-Quest was Jalen's hard, huge cock. I slid the first inch or two of the O-Quest into my sex. It had hurt a little the first time I'd tried it, a couple of months ago, but not now. I was naturally lubed up and definitely ready. I slid it out slightly, and then back, putting just a little more in, and I started breathing more evenly, in and out, and then another inch, and then the half U-shape was right next to my clit. In my mind, Jalen was kissing my neck and my ear, and talking dirty to me. "Oh, Rachel," he said in my fantasy, "I love the way you move. You're so beautiful. I can't get enough of you, my pretty girl."

"Don't stop touching me, Jalen," I whispered, and I started moving my hips in a slow circle, sliding the vibrator in and out of my sex, next to my clit then farther away, then back again.

I was so ready and wet I wasn't even sure I'd need to turn the vibrator on, but I clicked the button anyway. It was on the lowest setting, but even then, the sensations were amazing. I let out a low sigh, the waves of pleasure shooting through my body. There was no turning back now. I turned up the setting just a touch.

Oh, wow. That wasn't the right button. That changed the rhythm of the vibrator to a slow pulse. I tried to spread my legs, but my panties were tangled around my ankles, and I couldn't move them as far apart as I wanted to. *Ugh.* I kept my ankles together and spread my knees, but that changed the angle of something inside of me, and it wasn't nearly as good. I wasn't hitting the right spot with the vibrator anymore.

"Dammit, Jalen," I mumbled under my breath. "Why did you have to ask me out? Why did you have to be so goddamned intelligent and kind? Why does your ass have to be so goddamned perfect? And why did I have to mess everything up? Why aren't you fucking me in your car right now?"

I kicked at the panties, and finally they released their hold on one of my ankles. I changed my knees back to the way they were. Yes, that was the spot, right there. "Oh, Jalen," I said, "you dirty boy, making me so hot for you. Alicia doesn't get you going like this, does she? Even though she's got the perky tits and the *Cosmo* cover-girl body, you like me best, don't you, my love?"

"Yes, my sweet girl," Jalen said in my mind. I pictured his powerful arms wrap around me, his manly, rough hands roaming all over my body, squeezing my big ass one moment, fondling my full breasts the next. I fumbled for the buttons on the vibrator and this time I succeeded in kicking it up a notch in intensity. But I hit both buttons at the same time, and the slow pulse became a rhythm: two strong, sudden bursts of vibration and then one low hum, intensifying and backing off two or three times before it went back to the bursts.

"I can't believe I'm lucky enough to be inside you," fantasy-Jalen said into my ear, as I felt his breath, his hands, his cock. I pretended that I reached underneath his cock and cupped his balls, fondling them. I'd barely given his balls three gentle squeezes when I felt him start to convulse. "Oh, my girl," he said, "I'm filling you up, baby, I'm making you mine."

Then I was coming too, and my hand slipped slightly, bumping the half U-shape of the vibrator directly onto my clit. The fantasy turned up the volume knob on my pleasure. My previous sessions with the vibrator had been good, but this one with fantasy-Jalen in my head, his strong arms around me, his soft skin, his deep, intense eyes—it was transcendent. I squeezed my eyes shut tightly, and all I saw was Jalen's cock, erect and throbbing around my shimmering body as the waves crashed through me, the half U-shape buzzing on my clit.

It seemed like forever until the waves subsided, and I finally turned the vibrator off and exhaled all the way. My skin was tingling from the orgasm. It was not the first one I'd ever experienced, but before my daring purchase of the vibrator, I'd made do with the pulsating shower head.

Once I'd finally caught my breath, I pulled the vibrator out. I didn't want to put it away without a thorough cleaning, for sure, but I couldn't be stealthy enough to wash it off in the bathroom without my dad hearing me and then asking me what I was doing. That would lead to a horrible conversation, and I don't know if I'd be more embarrassed about it or if he would. I listened for a moment and heard him rattling around in the kitchen.

A couple of tissues from my nightstand would have to do. I wiped off the O-Quest as well as I could and then put it back in my drawer. I'd clean it properly the next day.

Laying back down and pushing the comforter off myself,

I only had the sheet over me. I had worked up a bit of a sweat through that self-love session, and the feel of the sheets on my naked skin still felt novel.

I was still buzzing as if I'd had too much coffee, but I could also feel my blood pressure go down and my heartbeat continue to return to normal. I rearranged the blankets and pillows around me, putting one of my large pillows down parallel to my body, from the small of my back to the backs of my thighs, pretending it was Jalen pressing his body against me, wrapping his arms around me, keeping me safe.

Reminiscing about our first date made feel embarrassed that I wasn't able to get what I wanted. Apparently, things hadn't gotten any better or less awkward for me. I still have trouble asking for what I want from Jalen, even though I have his ring around my finger and his last name.

On my own for dinner, again, I don't feel like making anything complicated. I find some linguine in the pantry and a jar of red sauce. I throw some olive oil in a pan and sauté some zucchini and some button mushrooms while the noodles cook.

In the wine rack in the guest room closet, there's a bottle of zinfandel from a couple of years before. Jalen and I bought it when we took a trip to Sonoma. It's not Jalen's favorite—zins are little heavy for his taste—but it's perfect for tonight. I open up the bottle, and then I dump the jar of sauce in the veggies. Two minutes later I've got dinner.

Holding my breath to balance everything, I carry the pasta and my full wine glass to the coffee table in the family room. I turn on the television, ready to get into another series. I don't really see anything that appeals to me, though. I wind up rewatching a couple of episodes of one of my favorite comedies that I watched in college, and I'm surprised to see that it hasn't aged very well. Some of the jokes fall flat.

No, that's not why I can't get into the TV show. It's that I'm totally preoccupied. I'm tired of Jalen traveling and of Jalen being too exhausted when he's home to have a real relationship with me. Now, on top of that, I'm too worried about what his ex-girlfriend will do when I'm not there with my little, distracting red sweater.

I get up from the couch after the second episode and then pour myself a third—fourth?—glass of wine. The cheap and easy pasta dinner was surprisingly satisfying. I check the time. It's almost seven.

I don't know when Jalen will be home. It could be any minute now, but it could be another few hours. My luck, it will probably be later.

This is just so unfair.

I take a long drink of the wine and I have to pee.

Sitting on the toilet a few minutes later, I look up and catch a glimpse of myself in the mirror.

Jesus. I look *terrible.* My hair is totally messed up, and my makeup, twelve hours after application, isn't helping matters. I wipe and flush and stand up and then go closer to the mirror.

Maybe it's seeing Alicia after all these years. She looks so young and so fit even though she's birthed two kids. And I look thirty-five and not-so-fit. It *is* kind of a trip seeing her again, and having all that hurt and unresolved anger come up again. I close my eyes and see her face in the halls at Montrose High as she sneers and calls me a dirty whore. *Yeesh.* That pain is still fresh.

I leave the bathroom and go sit down on the sofa and take another sip of zin. For fuck's sake, I'm so wound up about this that I'm not even enjoying this velvety zinfandel, with its hints of nutmeg, cedar, and chocolate. This is one of those wines I like so much I usually shush other people when I drink it.

My phone buzzes on the coffee table. It's from Jalen.

Alicia wants to go over my five biggest accounts tonight
I tried to beg off but she insisted
I'm sorry I'll be home by 10

Then he sends me a picture from the restaurant. It's a selfie. He's in his light gray suit with the subtle black pinstripes. He's wearing a black dress shirt and the silvery-blue tie that I bought him on my vacation to SoCal with my college roommate Gina. *Mmm, he looks good*, and it's not just because I haven't had sex with him in a while. This is him at his most tasty.

His face is contorted in annoyance. Alicia is behind him, facing the side. She is clearly absorbed in her phone. Jalen has his left hand up near his shoulder. He's flipping her off, but at an angle where she can't see his extended middle finger. I laugh.

I'm really sorry I will try to make it up to you

I text him back.

If I'm asleep, wake me up when you get home

All right, Alicia Parker Hawthorne, screw you and screw this pity party. I top off my wine and go upstairs.

I don't need to do anything particularly special to keep Jalen's eye from wandering, especially in comparison to Alicia, but I have no doubt that Alicia will try *something* with him. Maybe brushing against his arm, maybe sitting a little too close.

When Jalen gets home, I want to be the best version of myself I can be. I don't want to talk to him about how we haven't connected in the months since he's been traveling to Zurich. I don't want to talk to him about how lonely I've been. I *definitely* don't want to talk about the smutty shifter romance stories that I've written. Jeez, I think I might die from embarrassment if he found out about those. Certainly wouldn't be great if he found out about those while we were having this dry spell.

The dry spell ends tonight.

Maybe it's the three glasses of wine talking, but I'll be in full seduction mode when Jalen gets home. If Alicia is sitting too close to him, touching his arm, "accidentally" brushing his knee when she sits down, I'll go farther than that. And Jalen will be with someone he finds much more attractive than Alicia. I'll treat this like we're going out for Jalen's birthday.

I walk into my closet.

Hmm. Maybe not so much like we're going *out* for Jalen's birthday as we're staying *in* for his birthday.

I open the second from bottom drawer, and in the back, I find a couple of pieces of lingerie. There's a black chemise, all satiny, and a sheer babydoll. I don't know. I want to meet him downstairs as soon as he comes in from the garage, and I'd feel weird sitting around in lingerie. I'd have to stream the *Fifty Shades* movies or something.

No, that doesn't feel right.

Neither does dressing up in fancy clothes. I've got an ankle-length red dress with a high-cut slit up one leg, and spaghetti straps that shows off a ton of cleavage. I need to wear it with a strapless, but Jalen always says I look good in it. It accentuates all the right curves on me.

But come on. That dress is pretty much right out of a 1940s gumshoe movie. For that look to work half as well as I want it to, I need a fur boa and Jalen in an overcoat and fedora, cigarette smoke swirling around our heads.

What else can I do?

Hmm. I turn to Jalen's side of the closet. Maybe I can get inspiration there.

He'll get home in that fantastic gray suit, of course. I'm not sure he has anything in his closet that I find more sexy than that. There are a few costumes we have, mostly at my behest. I quite like him dressing up for Halloween in something sexy. I got him to be a sexy schoolteacher once. He had the fake round glasses, and a tight oxford shirt with the sleeves torn off, accentuating his powerful arms. He had a pocket protector with a bunch of pens stuck in it, which I guess was part nerd too—and it agreed with the nerd fetish I had in high school and college. I insisted on these skinny dress pants which were much too tight, not only on his muscular legs, but also around the crotch.

The only way I could get him to agree to wear that outfit to the Halloween party was for me to wear the sexy equivalent: a short plaid skirt and a tight white shirt, tied underneath my large breasts, along with a short tie attached to a collar that Velcroed around my neck. I wore black Mary Janes and white stockings that ended just above the knee, but a good three inches below the hem of my skirt.

There's also a sexy construction worker costume for him, hanging in the back. The orange shorts are so short and tight on him he looks like a male go-go dancer when he wears it. *Mmm, I want to bite his tight ass in that outfit.* Unfortunately, as good as the construction worker outfit looked on him, my outfit wasn't quite so successful at lowering his inhibitions. My costume had a tight white tank top that showed off my boobs, but the bright orange vest hid them, and my jean shorts and work boots were more realistic than sexy. It certainly didn't get the same positive reaction from him as the schoolgirl uniform had.

I walk out of our closet, taking another sip of wine, and spot the clock. 7:17 p.m. Oh man, what am I doing? I won't be in a sexy outfit or costume or lingerie for Jalen for the next three hours. He says he'll be home by ten, but I know that Alicia will try to keep him out as late as possible, just to make me angry.

Well, Alicia, it won't work. I'll be waiting for Jalen in a sexy outfit, and I'll be fucking him five minutes after he gets home.

But I won't get in the outfit now.

I wander around the house. What will I do for the next three hours? I suppose I could see what movies are on Netflix, or watch another couple of hours of old comedies.

Hmm. Maybe I'll work on another one of my sexy shifter

stories. That should definitely get me in the mood. It probably needs a little editing, anyway.

I walk into the office and wake up the laptop.

There's one story that I wrote based on Jalen's time at Arrowhead University, when he was the starting power forward on their basketball team. The basketball scholarship was how he got through school.

Although our first date had been awful, the aftermath wasn't all bad. I learned a lot about my body in the weeks after he and I went out. I often found myself fantasizing about Jalen. Learning exactly when in the masturbatory sessions to turn the vibrator from the slow pulse to the high buzz. Figuring out that I liked a pillow under the small of my back when I was getting myself off. Feeling embarrassed when I heard Mom tell Dad to just ignore the sounds coming from my bedroom because it was better that I was figuring this stuff out on my own, rather than fumbling through it in the backseat of some strange boy's car.

As I opened my story in Microsoft Word, I recalled the weeks after our first date—and my freshman year in college.

DOMINATING THE WOLFPACK

*E*ven though I knew I had a low chance of success, I tried to position myself in places where Jalen would run into me. I knew that he'd still liked my body. If I could just get him to try once more, things might go differently. I would smile warmly when he'd pass, and then I'd devolve into misery when he walked away.

Elaine shook her head. "It really went that badly?"

I sank against the lockers. "Yes. I couldn't talk about anything. The date was just one long uncomfortable silence."

"But he didn't talk either. Maybe he's feeling the same way." Elaine leaned against the wall and tapped her chin thoughtfully. "You know, the two of you might have to spend a few hours just getting all the physical stuff out of your system before you can have a real conversation."

I tilted my head. "What? Physical stuff out of our system? What—"

"I'm talking about *sex*, Rachel. You and Jalen are so hot for each other the air shimmers around you. A few hours between the sheets should probably get your tongues untied." Elaine smirked and folded her arms. "Unless your tongues are too busy doing other things to get untied."

I pushed myself off the bank of lockers and rolled my eyes. "Please, bitch. That is *not* a thing. That's something that would only exist in a romantic comedy."

"Or a pornographic movie."

I crinkled my nose. "No, that's too much plot for a porno."

Elaine laughed. "I don't really care if you think it's a *thing* or not. It's what you have to do."

I leaned toward Elaine and lowered my voice. "I'm not sure I want to lose my virginity like that."

"Are you kidding? I would have *loved* to lose my virginity with someone who was as into me as Jalen is into you. Sure beats what happened with Steve."

"Oh, honey, Steve was just confused."

"He was trying to convince himself he was straight," Elaine said, "and don't change the subject. We're talking about you fucking Jalen so you can go on a decent date."

I scoffed. "No, *you're* talking about it. It's not meant to be."

"It is *totally* meant to be. You and Jalen are so cute together, for one thing. For another, I'm not kidding about the heat between the two of you. When you look at each other, I feel like I'm not old enough to watch. Like, viewer discretion is advised."

"Okay, I get it. Now can we please go home so I can do my calculus?"

"There's still a chance, Rachel. It'll require his dick in your mouth—"

"Elaine!"

"—but it's still a chance. And Rachel, my dear, true love *always* deserves another chance."

It had been a long time since then. I don't remember if that was right before I found out that Jalen had gone back to Alicia Parker, when I tried to forget about Jalen in earnest. I know by the time we got back from Christmas break that Jalen and Alicia had broken up again. I never got up the nerve to ask him on another date, and I *certainly* never got the nerve to ask him to shove me up against the wall outside Mrs. Landis's history class, pull up my skirt, and fuck me until I came.

Although that did become my go-to fantasy with the O-Quest for about a week.

Around this time, I heard that Jalen got his acceptance letter to play basketball at Arrowhead University on a full ride. Some of his friends made fun of him for ditching the greater Phoenix area for Southern California, but Jalen was smart to get away from Phoenix. The summers were getting so hot the airplanes couldn't land at Sky Harbor.

I didn't say anything to Jalen directly, but I was also going to California. Not to Arrowhead, but to UC Irvine. It had a great computer science program. One of the professors there was the "mother of project management software," and I was getting weak in the knees at the possibility of her teaching me the ins and out of Work Breakdown Structures and Project Life Cycles.

As a freshman, Jalen became his team's starting power forward. One of the first games they played was against the University of Nevada, Reno. That early in the season, many of the major college leagues were off, so the game was nationally televised. He set a school record with 56 points, and nabbed 12 rebounds and 10 assists. He was *always* around the ball.

I didn't follow college sports a lot, but I was flipping channels on the TV in the common room that day when I saw Jalen's face, driving down the line, two defenders guarding him. He flipped the ball nonchalantly to a teammate who dunked the ball powerfully, the whole rim and backboard bending.

"With his eighth assist," the overexcited television announcer said, "Jalen Jefferson is completely dominating the Wolfpack."

Oh my. Completely dominating the wolfpack.

I didn't know at the time that the Wolfpack was Nevada's mascot, but that one phrase got my motor running. I could be forgiven for my thoughts immediately turning to teen werewolf romances, which were all the rage at the time. What I might not have been forgiven for was going over to my boyfriend's dorm room later that night. I hadn't yet lost my virginity, but I planned to strip, climb on top of him, and pretend he was Jalen.

The boyfriend, a mechanical engineering major named Ty, was a nice enough guy, although way too interested in Texas Hold'em. We'd been dating a couple of weeks. The reason we hadn't been together that Saturday afternoon was that he was watching a national poker tournament and I'd rather watch paint dry.

After the Arrowhead/Nevada game was over, I was restless and hornier than I'd been in a long time. Hornier than I'd been, in fact, since the night of my first date with Jalen.

When I knocked on Ty's door, I was already planning how I could take off my panties without having to make conversation with him.

Ty answered the door and I stepped toward him and kissed him. I snaked my tongue into his mouth and pushed up my body against his. He wrapped his arms around me, and after a moment, he dropped his hands to my ass and squeezed.

With my eyes closed, I kept kissing him, grinding my hips in slow circles, getting friction against his thigh. Ty's cock hardened beneath his jeans and nudged against my belly, and I moaned.

When we broke from the kiss, Ty gasped for breath, and to me he looked more scared than horny. *Can I really lose my virginity to this guy while I pretend he's Jalen?*

After all, Ty was not a man who could dominate a wolfpack.

He smiled, running one hand through his hair and clearing his throat. "Hey, Rachel."

"Hey, Rachel," another voice inside the dorm room said.

"I'm watching the tournament with Evan," he said.

"Hey, Evan," I called. Then leaning forward, I whispered, "Wasn't your roommate going home for the weekend?"

"He was, but his ride bailed on him. We're just hanging out."

"You doing anything later tonight?" I moved my hand to his chest.

Immediately the fantasy of Jalen fucking me against the wall outside the History classroom sprang into my head. Feeling Jalen's urgent thrusts in and out of me, his rough hands on me, while I reached a hand blindly behind me to touch his muscular chest or shoulders or abs. The image was so powerful, so vivid, that it seemed real. It seemed like I could wish Jalen there in that tiny beige dorm room. I wasn't sure it wouldn't work. I was staring at my hand on Ty's chest. I looked up at him, and confusion clouded his face.

"What did you just say?"

I raised my other hand to my mouth and lightly bit my index finger in what I hoped was a sexy way. "I was hoping you'd be free tonight."

"Tonight?"

"We've been dating for a couple of weeks. Maybe we could, uh, take the next step."

He looked nervous and unsure. *Oh no, did he not want to?*

"Uh—no, it's not that. You called me 'Jason.'"

Oh crap. I'd called him *Jalen* without realizing it. I had to get him out of my head. I wouldn't spend my whole freshman year hung up on a guy from high school. My mind raced.

"My computer science class. JavaScript Object Notation —*jay-ess-oh-en*. It's—it's a language we're just starting to learn. I just learned the Next Object command. Nerdy, I know, wanting us to, uh, have a special night together, and the first thing out of my mouth is a programming language."

He laughed with relief. "Sure. Give me just another hour or so till they get through the final table. I'll give you a call."

I unbuttoned my top two buttons, showing quite a bit of cleavage. "Maybe you don't have to watch the final table."

He looked stricken. "I mean, it's just another hour. I'll call you when it's over, and then I can come to your place."

He glanced at Evan, who was sitting in a desk chair, engrossed in the poker game on the TV.

Oh.

Ty didn't look at me and my curves the way Jalen did. I'd seen that look on guys' faces before. He thought I was pretty. He probably even thought I was sexy. But more than anything, he was worried that his friends would make fun of him for dating me.

It's funny. Since Jalen, the hottest guy in school, looked at me the way he did, it didn't really matter that this guy—who couldn't hold a candle to Jalen any day of the week—thought I wasn't worth going out with. Even if I was smart and funny and nerdy enough to hold a conversation about most of the nonpoker related stuff he was into. Because he didn't think his friends would find me attractive, even if *he* did.

Your loss, pal.

"Sure," I said, a smile plastered to my face. "Try not to be too long, Ty. I'd hate to have to start without you."

As I walked back to my dorm, I knew I'd have to break up with him, but he wasn't making it all that difficult for me.

In fact, I *could* start without him. I wasn't willing to wait until he was done watching television with his roommate. He probably assumed that for some reason I was desperate for his cock.

My roommate Gina had gone out with friends after the game and I didn't expect her back until really late. So I got out my trusty O-Quest and pictured Jalen in bed with me, taking charge with me like he had in the game against Nevada.

Even though Ty had said he'd call me after the poker

game, he didn't interrupt my fantasy with a phone call that night. A few days later, I bumped into Ty in the campus commons. It gave me the perfect opportunity to tell him our relationship wasn't working out.

Ty looked at me like I was crazy. "You're mad at me? I didn't forget your birthday or anything."

I shrugged. "I know. But it's pretty obvious we want different things." *For instance, I want to put Jalen's huge cock inside me, and you'd probably be pretty upset if I did that.*

The look of confusion on his face was deeper than the one he wore Saturday night. "Is this because I didn't call you after the poker game?"

"Well—kind of. I mean, I made it pretty clear that I was ready to have sex with you. And you blew me off."

"My roommate didn't have anything to do. I couldn't just leave."

I nodded. "I get it, Ty. Look, maybe I'm not your type. That's cool. Better I know that after a couple of weeks than after a couple of years."

"No, that's not it at all." His eyes drank me in as he looked me up and down. Yep, I was right. He wanted me, but he didn't want his friends to know.

"Thank you, Ty, but we're just not right for each other. Sorry." I smiled sweetly, and he narrowed his eyes, and then he turned and walked away.

Gina spent that night with a new beau who lived in an off-campus apartment. I took the O-Quest out from the bottom drawer, knowing that I didn't have anything going on until my chemistry lab at eight in the morning.

That night, for the first time, I fantasized about Jalen as a transforming magic creature.

He dominated the wolfpack, and not just on the court. My fantasies were rife with werewolves, howling as Jalen's alpha-wolf cock pumped in and out of me, the full moon illuminating my curvy, naked body, as Jalen howled and filled me, again and again, over and over.

Tonight, as Jalen is out with his ex-girlfriend and new boss right after his last two-week-long business trip, I remember that dream, that whole sequence of events, and I put pen to paper—well, fingers to computer keyboard, anyway.

I'd written quite a bit in *The Princess and the Unicorn*, but I'm stuck. I can't figure out how to get the princess back home. Every time I try to return her to her parents, she runs back to Jalen the unicorn and has sex with him. I sigh, and then I have an idea. I start writing a scene where she has sex with Prince Jalen in unicorn form. After about forty-five minutes and a thousand words, I wonder if I'm getting the details right. Yes, I know, unicorns aren't real creatures, so it doesn't matter. I still search online for unicorn erotica and I spend the next several hours fascinated by several online stories of varying quality. Mostly unrealistic plots and poor characterization, but a couple of them have some really hot sex scenes. I finish my research, a little more enlightened, and I open up the file of *The Princess and the Unicorn*.

Ugh. I don't feel like continuing this story tonight. I need to change too many things about the story, and it overwhelms me.

The night I broke up with Ty, though, suddenly appears in my head, along with the phrase *completely dominating the wolfpack*, and I open a different file, one titled *An American Werewolf in Phoenix*. When I started the story a month ago, it wasn't a name I was planning to keep, but at least the working title got me started.

And now, killing time before Jalen gets home from dinner with his new boss and old ex-girlfriend, I start to read.

AN AMERICAN WEREWOLF IN PHOENIX, PART I

*I*t was a sunny and calm morning in the Phoenix suburb of Montrose. The town was still mostly asleep at six o'clock on a Saturday. The sun wasn't peeking over the horizon yet, and the full moon was quickly fading as the sky lightened, the first fingers of orange light casting its warm glow above the mountains.

It would be a hot day, not atypical for late April. The temperature was already above ninety degrees.

(I'd debated calling the protagonist Jalen Jefferson, but I had just called the unicorn *Jalen*, so I decided to go with the more pedestrian *Jeff*.)

A young man named Jeff, slender but strong—what most people would call *wiry*—was training for a marathon, and he was already in the seventh mile of his ten-mile run.

He turned left down Catamaran Avenue—strange how a landlocked suburb like Montrose had so many streets named after kinds of boats—and crossed Glendale Boulevard.

On the other side of the thoroughfare, Catamaran Avenue became more like a country road. There was no sidewalk, only a dirt path. Jeff liked running on the packed soil, so much more comfortable than the hard asphalt. He had burned up the trails on the cross-country team in high school, and with any luck, he'd qualify for the Boston Marathon next year.

He kept the woods on his left and turned up the music in his earbuds.

There'd been rumors about the woods, a thousand acres of scrub pine and ironwoods that weren't uncommon in this hot climate. How there were strange creatures living in them. There'd been some odd deaths the last couple of years, mostly people who'd been traveling in the woods at night—a few homeless people, a pair of teenaged lovers, and a man who'd escaped the police after a high-speed chase.

But these were all after-midnight deaths, and they were all deep in the woods. The escapee's body had been found over two miles into the scrub, and there were no drag marks, either. So Jeff figured he was safe here, running next to the road.

The wounds on all the victims were similar. Sharp canine teeth and incisors, flaying the neck and the upper thighs, seeming to go for both the carotid and the femoral, with huge losses of blood for each of the victims.

But Jeff wasn't thinking about the arteries of the dead people. He was concentrating on the marathon. He looked at his watch, moving at a good, strong pace. He might be able to shave over a minute off his ten-mile time. Training in the heat of Phoenix would prepare him decently for the possible mugginess of Boston in April. But first he'd have to finish a qualifying marathon in less than three hours—probably more like two hours fifty-eight minutes. If he ran as well as he knew he could, if he stayed focused, and had a little bit of luck in the field, he'd get a qualifying time.

He took his phone out of his armband and switched to a faster song, and as the downbeat crashed at the same instant his right foot landed, he started accelerating. He breathed in. Even though it was hot, the air felt good in his lungs. Fresh, dry, full of oxygen. Jeff smiled. He'd hit his stride, and he was confident that nothing could come between him and a good two minutes off his fastest time so far.

Then he heard a thunderous roar behind him, and as he turned his head, everything went dark.

Jeff was lucky that the attack took place so close to the edge of the road. Two hunters in a pickup truck stopped when they saw a hairy beast crouched over the supine form of the fallen man.

Both the passenger and driver jumped out of the pickup and drove the beast off with shotgun blasts. They pulled Jeff into the bed of their truck, as he was bleeding from the neck, and took him to the hospital.

It was touch-and-go. Jeff languished in a coma, the wounds stubbornly refusing to heal, but he was stable enough to be transferred from the emergency room to the ICU. That morning, neurologist Rachel Bennet read the file on her new patient and was stumped.

As the young, curvy doctor walked into the room to see Jeff for the first time, Dr. Bennet kept staring at the charts on her tablet, puzzling over the odd numbers and the strange results from his blood tests. There must have been some mistake. Perhaps the blood had gotten tainted, or perhaps the machines were off. Nothing made sense, though. Phoenix General had not only the most professional staff she'd ever encountered, but also policies and procedures in place with many checks and balances to make sure that these sorts of errors never happened. Still, mistakes were bound to get through every once in a while. Nothing was perfect.

She looked up from her tablet to Jeff's face—and gasped. He was fantastically handsome, even in his comatose state. She couldn't believe it. The man in the hospital bed in front of her had a strong but not sharp jawline, soft cheekbones, and just the kind of lithe yet muscled build that drove her wild. The universe was so cruel. He was her physical ideal, yet it didn't look like he would make it, crazy blood test results or not.

She sighed. It wasn't just his good looks and hot body either. She'd read his background, and she could feel in her bones a kindness and an openness about him that was increasingly uncommon in men her age. All deaths were tragedies, but his would be particularly heartbreaking.

Over the next few days, in spite of Dr. Bennet's pessimism, Jeff started to fight his way out of the illness. He exhibited some of the symptoms of blood poisoning, and Dr. Bennet noted that his body hair grew more rapidly than normal. He was still unconscious in the ICU, however. Although some signs pointed in a positive direction, Dr. Bennet still had little hope he'd recover, which, in some ways was worse. Living out your days in a hospital bed for years was not ideal. And Jeff was young, maybe in his late twenties, not only with his whole life ahead of him, but perhaps five decades of nothing but a coma.

She noted with some confusion that Jeff's body seemed to be getting stronger. The color wasn't draining from his face, nor was his muscle tone depleted. In fact, he seemed healthier. Five days after he came into the ICU, his biceps seemed larger to Dr. Bennet.

She shook her head. It had to be her mind playing tricks on her. He couldn't get more fit just lying comatose in a hospital bed.

The next day, she was sure his muscles were larger again, but that was impossible—wasn't it? She came back into his room with a measuring tape. Dr. Bennet put her hand on his arm and it felt... wonderful. Warm, inviting, like an emotional embrace. She cleared her throat and ran a hand through her honey blonde hair. Then, taking a deep breath and steeling herself, she wrapped the measuring tape around Jeff's left bicep. Just a touch under fifteen and one-half inches, about what she expected for a lithe, muscular man who was in marathon shape.

Dr. Bennet hesitated. Should she put these measurements in the system? She wasn't sure. If this was some sort of a phenomenon, she'd be remiss not to keep records. But if anyone were to ask her what she was doing, they'd assume she was crazy if she pointed out that Jeff's biceps were growing.

Which raised the question: were other parts of Jeff growing too?

She lifted the blanket and looked at Jeff's ankles and calves. She didn't know what Jeff's lower legs looked like when he came in, so she had nothing to compare them to. She touched his calf, and again felt the inviting warmth move up her arm. Clearing her throat and trying to ignore the sensation, she noted that his leg muscles were firm, as if he were flexing. She stole a glance at his face, but his eyelids were closed, and the steady, boring beeping of the monitor kept time.

What about his other muscles? His pectorals, his abdominals, his thighs, his glutes? He was a runner, certainly, so he had reason to be in good shape. What was the best way to get his gown off to measure the rest of his body? She took a step back and surveyed his form.

Oh, goodness.

He was tenting his hospital gown at the crotch. And it wasn't a pup tent, either.

How was this happening? Dr. Rachel Bennet was still young and had only seen three other patients who were in comas. Two of them were women, and the other was a man in his late eighties. She'd never seen a man so young in such a condition. She remembered her medical training, and that tumescence in the comatose sometimes mirrored that of people in deep REM sleep. It wasn't common, but there *was* a scientific explanation for it.

Dr. Bennet licked her lips. Perhaps she should just pull up his gown to his waist and perform some measurements. You know, to be thorough.

She slowly reached for Jeff's erect member that was straining the material of the gown—and then stopped, her fingers less than an inch from the tent.

Dr. Rachel Bennet shook her head and pulled her hand back. What was she doing? Jeff was a comatose patient and she was acting like a teenaged boy with a stolen password for a porn site. She had measured the bicep, and that was enough to see if something odd was happening with his musculature. She didn't need to see his chest or stomach. She didn't need to measure his upper thighs or get her hands so close to his manhood, huge and throbbing in spite of his condition. No matter how good-looking he was, no matter how much he fit her ideal physical specimen. No matter how delectably erect he might be, no matter that it had been months since she'd last gotten laid. No matter how wet her sex was, or how much she wanted him deep inside of her.

Dr. Bennet stood up and rearranged the blankets over him, disgusted with herself but still agonizingly horny. She couldn't stop fantasizing about Jeff and his tented hospital gown, the summit proudly popped up like a vulgar mountain.

That night, Dr. Bennet had three vivid dreams of riding Jeff's hard, pulsing cock. He was always on his back, his dick a near-perpendicular wonder. In the first dream, they were on her kitchen table, she was on her knees, thrusting her hips up and down. In the second dream, they lay on the bearskin rug at her friend's uncle's cabin in Colorado, with her squatting over his fat cock, facing away from him, using her leg muscles to raise and lower herself. And in the third and most vivid dream, she found herself in a pristine white room, Jeff lying on the floor, naked.

Dr. Rachel Bennet was in a sex swing, her legs high in stirrups, her sex positioned about a foot above his cock. She stayed stock-still for a few delicious, agonizing moments, until the swing began to dip and rise, spinning slowly. As it dipped, Jeff's cock entered Rachel's dripping wet pussy, and she moaned in pleasure. The swing spun faster as she slowly went up and down on his cock, and the white room became a blur. As she gained speed, the walls turned into a prism, and red, orange, green, and blue lights were visible in

Rachel's vision. As she closed her eyes in her dream, the colors stayed, only with a black backdrop instead of a white one. She was breathing heavier now, and felt her orgasm build, and build, and build, then finally release, as she shook violently in the swing. Her feet stuck stubbornly in the stirrups as her hips bucked, and her vaginal muscles pulsated around him.

That's when his cock finally went through its own release, covering Dr. Bennet's velvety walls with his cum. In this position, she felt his jizz drip out of her sex as he was still shooting his load into her, spinning in reverse now, as smaller orgasms continued to burst through her body.

When the spinning stopped, dream-Rachel opened her eyes, and so did the real Rachel Bennet, respected neurosurgeon, naked, wrapped up in her bedsheets, her juices flowing out of her sex. She blinked hard a few times before she realized that she didn't just have an orgasm in her dream, she had one in real life, too, and she felt her vaginal muscles pulse, as if a man's huge, hard cock had just been inside.

She sighed and looked at the bedside clock. 5:42 a.m. Time to wake up and go back to the hospital.

After Dr. Bennet got to work, she consulted with a couple of new patients. She was eager to see Jeff again, but wanted to stay professional. When she did her rounds, Jeff was her last patient. She measured his bicep again. Just a touch over fifteen and one-half inches. The same as yesterday. She was sure she had imagined the growth, although she couldn't help noticing that his whole body looked more toned.

She tapped on her tablet to enter the measurement—and no, that wasn't right. His bicep had measured a little *under* fifteen and one-half inches yesterday. Today it was a touch *over*.

She put down the tablet on the counter, and then threw back the blankets that had been covering Jeff's body. She immediately noticed his erection again. It seemed larger and harder than it had the day before, even covered by the hospital gown. The curvy neurosurgeon stood transfixed for a moment. She began to salivate, and a ripple of horror shot down her spine. This wasn't the way for a doctor to behave around her patient—any patient, much less a comatose one. But the desire to rip off Jeff's hospital gown and stroke his huge, throbbing cock was overwhelming. She could almost smell her own arousal. She knew she could easily lick the underside of Jeff's pulsating manhood, from where the shaft met his balls, all the way to the bottom of the corona.

She wondered how Jeff's precum would taste. She wondered how quickly a comatose Jeff would ejaculate, and how much stimulation it would take. Where would the stimulation be most effective? Some guys she'd dated liked their balls gently squeezed, some guys like a straight sucking, still others liked it when Dr. Bennet put their whole cock in her mouth. She didn't like that as much, but it was sometimes exciting to see the man's reaction to it. She wondered how hard his ejaculate would shoot out. Would his jizz spurt across the room, since he hadn't come for a couple of weeks? Or would the coma have weakened his motor neurons in Onuf's nucleus in his sacral spinal cord? Had the attack damaged the fibers projecting through the motor component of the pudendal nerve, and would the messages of arousal even reach the pelvic musculature? Had it adversely affected the bulbospongiosus muscle, the ischiocavernosus bilateral muscle, or even the external urethra?

"You fucking dirty bitch," Dr. Rachel Bennet whispered to herself, reaching out to test the pelvic musculature for herself.

Then she jumped away for the second time in as many days. What was she doing? She couldn't touch him like that. She breathed heavily. *Holy shit—that was really close*. This couldn't be happening.

Dr. Bennet took several steps back from the hospital bed and, as calmly as she could manage, walked out of the room and over to the nurse's station where Nurse Alicia sat behind the desk. Dr. Bennet steeled herself. Nurse Alicia was often unhelpful and surly, and she'd made Dr. Bennet look bad in front of the hospital administrators on more than one occasion. Other times, the nurse seemed to cower in the doctor's presence. Rachel had wanted to write Alicia up on more than one occasion, but all the other doctors said that the beautiful nurse was the most competent one in the entire hospital. It seemed the only time Alicia was ever anything less than helpful, insightful, and intelligent was when she had to assist Dr. Bennet.

The neurosurgeon wondered which Nurse Alicia she would be getting today.

"Alicia, you're assigned to Jeff D'Arcy in Room 7, correct?"

"That's right, Dr. Bennet."

"Do you have a moment? I'd like you to observe something. Perhaps there is a condition you've noticed during your time with him that will give me some additional data points."

"Certainly, Dr. Bennet."

Nurse Alicia followed Dr. Bennet tentatively into Jeff's room. The doctor turned and looked at the nurse. The young woman was jumpy and skittish today, not churlish and surly. Some of the staff around the hospital said the pretty nurse was jealous of the doctor's curvaceous figure. The head of the ICU even had to admonish Alicia for talking too much about the doctor's curvy form on one of Rachel's days off. Dr. Bennet suspected Alicia had some unresolved issues in her past. She'd overheard another nurse joke that Alicia had lost a previous boyfriend to the charms of a Junoesque woman, not unlike the doctor. Perhaps the poor young woman didn't have the emotional tools to deal with her feelings.

Dr. Bennet cleared her throat, and Nurse Alicia almost jumped out of her skin. "Nurse," the neurosurgeon said, pointedly ignoring the jumpy woman's reaction, "have you observed anything unusual in this patient? Especially over, say, the last couple of days?"

"Anything unusual?" Nurse Alicia asked, her voice quivering. "I'm not sure what you mean."

"Physically, if I need to clarify. Anything physically on Mr. D'Arcy that you've noticed?"

"Um... well, I guess he's really handsome. You know, hot. Good-looking."

Doctor Rachel Bennet smiled. "Yes, Alicia, I know what all those terms mean."

"Sorry." The nurse looked miserably at her shoes.

"Have you noticed anything about his muscle mass?"

She looked out of the corner of her eye at Dr. Bennet. "I don't know what you mean. I told you he was hot."

"You haven't noticed any change in his musculature? His tone, perhaps the size of his arm muscles?"

Alicia pursed her lips, which made her lips appear pale and thin. "I don't know."

Dr. Bennet pulled out the tape measure from her coat pocket. "I measured Mr. D'Arcy's left bicep yesterday. It was nearly fifteen and one-half inches. Today, it is slightly *more* than fifteen and one-half inches. You haven't noticed any change in the size of his muscles?"

"No?" Alicia said, wincing.

"Have you and the other nurses been attending to Mr. D'Arcy's body appropriately? Warm water, mild soap, patting dry with towels, making sure he's not exhibiting signs of skin ulcers or bedsores?"

"Of course, doctor."

"And has anything, um, stood out to you in particular?"

"Stood out, Doctor Bennet?" She took a cautionary step back. "I'm not sure I understand."

The doctor pulled back the covers from Jeff's body with a flourish. His erection was still hard and proud, pushing against the fabric of the hospital gown. Nurse Alicia gasped. "Oh, doctor!" She stared at the tented gown as if she'd never seen a rudely erect penis before.

"Yes," Dr. Rachel Bennet affirmed. "Our patient has developed an erection, Nurse Alicia. I found him in a similar state when I came in yesterday. It was the first time I'd noticed it, but, as you know, comas can mimic deep REM sleep. Sexual arousal during sleep cycles—and in comatose patients—isn't unheard of. Not that common, but not a cause for concern in and of itself."

Nurse Alicia nodded, still staring.

"I come in here two days in a row and find him in the same state," Dr. Bennet said, "and I wonder if this is an ongoing issue. Tell me, Nurse Alicia, have you noticed that Mr. D'Arcy's penis being erect today or yesterday?"

"I—uh, no, Doctor," Alicia murmured. "I'm sure I would have noticed. Especially as I personally bathed him yesterday evening."

Dr. Bennet nodded. Alicia was being cagey and quick to respond, which worried the doctor. "Can you be completely sure?"

"I'm positive, Doctor. No erection last evening when I washed Mr. D'Arcy's penis." She went silent and looked at the ground. "I'm not sure if you're accusing me of something."

"No, no," Dr. Bennet said, patting Nurse Alicia's hand. "I was just concerned that it may have been erect since yesterday, or perhaps longer. Might be a sign of a serious blood circulation issue. Make sure you keep an eye on it, okay?"

"Yes, Doctor."

"All right. That's all for me this morning, Nurse Alicia. Thanks."

She turned and walked out of the room, leaving the blanket around Mr. D'Arcy's legs.

She was halfway down the hall when Nurse Alicia stuck her head out of the ICU room. "Doctor Bennet! Mr. D'Arcy has lost his erection!"

The ICU hallway was fortunately empty, but Dr. Rachel Bennet scowled at Nurse Alicia. "Lower your voice," she grunted, walking back to the room. "Shouting about a comatose man's erection down the hall is a privacy violation.

We could get sued so fast you wouldn't know which way was up."

Nurse Alicia blushed.

Dr. Bennet walked in the room and Jeff's gown was pushed up to his waist, his naked penis completely uncovered, but also unashamedly and unabashedly hard, sticking up about ten degrees from vertical toward his stomach. A glistening drop of precum sat proudly on the tip of his cock.

Oof. She felt a nearly magnetic pull to Jeff's rigid, throbbing member as she gasped, trying to catch her breath and using all of her willpower to keep her hands by her sides. "Nurse Alicia," she groaned, feeling erotic heat sweep over her body, "You shouted down the hall that his erection had subsided."

"Honestly, Dr. Bennet, I thought it had!" Nurse Alicia wrung her hands. "I don't know what happened!"

"You wanted to embarrass me," Dr. Bennet said. "I should write you up for this."

"No, Dr. Bennet, please don't!" Nurse Alicia begged.

"You've undermined my authority," the doctor seethed, desperately trying to tear her eyes away from Jeff's engorged cock. "It's disrespectful and insubordinate, and I won't have it."

"I'd never do that," Nurse Alicia blurted.

"You'd never do that?" Dr. Rachel Bennet said incredulously. "You've treated me poorly from day one of my tenure here. I've felt unwelcome. You treat me like I'm stupid. I've *never* felt as low as I do when I finish my shift when you're on the floor. You're telling me you'd *never* undermine my authority?"

Nurse Alicia had tears streaming down her face. "I'm so

sorry, Dr. Bennet. You remind me of a girl who stole my boyfriend in high school. I need this job. I guess I couldn't handle my feelings."

"It looks like you still can't," the curvy neurosurgeon said icily.

Nurse Alicia's face crumpled, and she ran out of the room, choking back sobs.

Dr. Bennet felt a stab of guilt. "Wait—Alicia—"

But Nurse Alicia was too far down the hall.

Dr. Bennet sighed at the unexpected turn of events. At least the beautiful nurse's escape had broken the spell that Jeff's huge erection had on her. She turned back to the hospital bed. The uncovered cock, vulgar in its rigidity, stared accusingly at her.

"Oh, shut up," she snapped. "As if *you're* any help." She grabbed the bottom hem of the hospital gown at Jeff's waist to cover him up again and then hesitated.

Not only was his penis large, but it was smooth, the skin unblemished, a slight upward curve to it—and quite, well, *attractive*. She'd certainly been sent unbidden pictures of much uglier ones before she'd given up on online dating apps.

Another positive aspect of Jeff's member: it also was the source of jealousy and frustration for Dr. Bennet's nemesis. Human nature being what it is, Dr. Bennet both felt guilty *and* reveled in the discomfort and embarrassment that the Nurse Alicia felt.

Dr. Bennet found herself pausing, not wanting to tear her eyes away from the young man's hard cock. The bottom of his abdominal muscles were also visible, the lower two of a perfect six-pack. She allowed the back of her hand to lightly touch his penis, as her knuckles brushed against his stomach.

She closed her eyes. She'd been on a single date with a man this perfect in high school, but she clammed up and couldn't even talk to him during the date. Now, she'd found another man just as handsome and cut, and *he* was the one who couldn't talk, this time due to a medical condition.

She forced herself to pull the gown back over his naked lower body and then arranged the blankets on top of him, and left the room.

The world was so cruel sometimes.

&

I finish reading the chapter. I liked the part about Dr. Bennet fantasizing about getting in the sex swing and spinning on top of Jeff's cock. I remember doing some online research about sex swings. First, I found out where you can procure sex swings—spoiler alert, a lot more places than you think—and then I watched some instructional videos.

I came really close to buying one of the spinning swings, but I didn't trust myself to competently install the ceiling mount. It wasn't a job for Jalen, either—he's fairly handy, but probably not I-trust-you-to-be-able-to-suspend-four-hundred-pounds-from-the-ceiling handy. That felt to me like it required some sort of certificate. Jalen's older brother was a woodworker and a licensed electrician, but I sure don't want him knowing we installed a sex swing. Although it might be something I'd want to rub in his smug wife's face.

I pictured Jalen coming home from Zurich, exhausted from having been in transit for twenty-four hours, calling my name, and then opening the bedroom door to see me in the swing, hanging between the foot of the bed and the wall, naked, my body begging for him to take me.

The night that I researched the scene, my mouse hovered over the *Buy Now* button. The swing even qualified for Prime shipping. It had over a hundred five-star reviews.

But the cost. It was a little more money than I wanted to spend, and I couldn't justify the purchase. I'd never been in a sex swing before, and to my knowledge Jalen hadn't used one either. I hadn't even brought it up to him, not even hypothetically. We considered ourselves adventurous in the bedroom, sure, but when you start having to worry about load-bearing ceiling beams, it's a whole different conversation than whether or not you want to use the fur-lined handcuffs.

That night, though, I chickened out. And before Jalen got home two days later, I'd removed it from the online shopping cart too.

But maybe surprising him with something big like a sex swing was exactly the kind of grandiose, over-the-top gesture our marriage needed.

For a moment I debate calling someone to install the swing. Is having a strange guy in my house installing a sex swing in the bedroom better than getting Jalen's older brother to do it? I don't know. Maybe Jalen's brother is the better choice. Maybe Theo wouldn't make fun of Jalen and me. Maybe the sex swing would be bragging rights for Jalen, as sophomoric as that might sound. *Jalen's wife is so fucking hot for him that she's installing a goddamn sex swing while he's gone.* Yeah, that's right, Theo. Let's see Yvette up the ante on *that*. She might not have issues with her uterus like I do, but I'll be begging my husband for a gravity-free fucking tonight while you're still cleaning up your preschooler's toys in the living room.

I sigh. When will I take control of my own happiness? Before he traveled constantly, and before we knew we'd have trouble conceiving, Jalen and I fucked like rabbits. The honeymoon didn't stop when we got back from Hawaii. We screwed in every room in our apartment in Orange County, and then after we moved up here, the apartment in Midtown, and when we bought this house last year, we screwed in every room here, too. We did it before the furniture was brought in, even before the window coverings went up. Even though the trees blocked most of the sightlines to the street, but I came a little harder knowing that our neighbors were out there. If someone stood at just the right spot in the cul-de-sac, and looked up at just the right angle, they'd see Jalen and his tight, hard, glorious ass, or they'd see my curvy body riding on top of him, or they'd see Jalen run his fingers through my hair as I sucked him off.

I recalled meeting the neighbors when the moving truck arrived the next day—it was fun and a little bit naughty. The couple two doors down, a good-looking guy named Dante and his wife Kendra, who is even curvier than I am with a drop-dead gorgeous face, helped us carry some things in. They had invited us to the neighborhood barbecue. I looked at them and how white-bread they seemed. Kendra's dress was a little short, which she wasn't aware of, but the way Dante kept looking at her thighs and her ass, I knew *he* was aware of how little her dress covered. I caught Kendra's eye as she brought in an end table and carried it to the living room. She smiled brightly.

Jalen asked Dante what he did for a living.

"I just sold my software company," Dante said, "so I'm taking some time off, spending a lot of time with the kids, doing the stay-at-home dad thing."

"How old are your kids?"

"Aidan is seven, and Maggie's turning five next week. She's starting kindergarten in the fall."

"How about you?" Kendra asked. "You have children?"

"Not yet," I said, smiling. "But this neighborhood seems great to raise kids. We had a two-bedroom we were renting in Midtown."

Kendra smiled warmly and she and Dante shared a look I couldn't quite figure out. At the time, I wondered if they had seen Jalen and me screwing through the window.

Now, a year later, it's not Jalen and me having sex in front of an uncovered window, it's Kendra and Dante. Even though both of them are quite attractive, I'm not sure I was ready to watch the two of them going at it. I had come home after a dentist appointment in the late morning, and as I walked to get the mail, I saw them through the picture window of their living room, their curtains wide open. Kendra was on top of him, riding him for all he was worth. Part of me wanted to tear my eyes away, like Dr. Bennet wanted to be able to stop looking at Jeff's huge, erect, comatose cock. Another part of me wanted to press my nose to the outside of their picture window, my hand in my panties, getting myself off. And *another* part of me, the largest part, wanted Jalen to get home from Zurich, so I could ride him on the sofa in the living room, just like Kendra was riding Dante.

I snap back to the present, rereading the Jalen-as-a-werewolf story, and I won't lie, getting a little weirded out at myself by the part where I included Nurse Alicia in the scene. I guess I like the fact that Dr. Rachel Bennet has power over her. It felt like revenge for all the times she spread rumors about me, or knocked my books out of my hands, and just pretended she hadn't done any of it.

What the hell did Jalen ever see in her?

I mean, she *was* Cosmo-model beautiful. And, yeah, he was seventeen. I guess he can get a pass.

I also remember writing that part, and wondering where I should go with the scene. Should Dr. Bennet start sucking Jeff's cock right there in the hospital bed? Should Alicia walk in on the scene and start sucking him off too, each of the women taking a side of his cock? First of all, I'd *definitely* have to change Alicia's name if those characters had a three-way. No, that's a bridge too far. I was writing for *myself*. A double blowjob felt like a scene I'd put in for Jalen if he were to read it.

Just the thought of Jalen reading this put a tremor inside me. *Yeesh.* What if Jalen were to find this? I can't imagine what I would say if Jalen caught me writing these.

Oh, listen to me, Rachel Jefferson, mad proponent of Female Empowerment, saying *if Jalen caught me writing these.* It's not like I can't do whatever I want in my spare time, whether it's taking a cooking class without him, or attending a concert with my coworkers, or, in fact, writing dirty books about the two of us as thinly-veiled characters fucking the ever-loving bejeezus out of each other.

I know I'm not a prude. Not after what we did while we were in college, surely. Yes, he doesn't own me or my libido, or what I do when he's on business trips, but he wouldn't be *okay* with his wife writing smut about him like this. It's not like he wouldn't "allow" me to do it, not at all. I just think he'd be a little hurt. Maybe his ego would be bruised if he thought I needed sex swings and a pretty nurse to watch me fondle his erection. He and I align pretty closely on a lot of things, but maybe Jalen would get a little weirded out if his character is totally comatose while I—I mean, my character —fucks him. Fucks his character. If Dr. Bennet fucks Mr. D'Arcy.

He might also get weirded out if he reads the part about my character disciplining his ex-girlfriend's character. Maybe he'd think that I still have unresolved feelings about their relationship. Or *maybe* he'd expect that I'm hinting at a three-way, and he'd get totally turned on by it. Which would weird *me* out.

I *am* enjoying that Nurse Alicia is so unhappy and uncomfortable around Dr. Rachel Bennet. *Hmm. Maybe I do have some unresolved feelings about their relationship.*

I turn this over in my mind for a second, but shrug. It's not like I'm sending this off to an agent to try to get published. This is just for me, and for my hungry, needy pussy when my husband is nine time zones away... or when he's having dinner with his boss and ex-girlfriend.

I look at the clock. Almost nine o'clock. Plenty of time before Jalen gets here for me to shower and get ready for him.

COLLEGE TOUR

*T*he timing is perfect. I can take a shower, spend a decent amount of time on my hair, and still get into something sexy for Jalen when he walks through the door. I won't be waiting downstairs for him for hours, either, so maybe my outfit *can* be something in the lingerie category. The sheer babydoll is probably his favorite.

In the shower, I let the water cascade over my head and my face and I breathe in and out carefully and slowly so I won't get water up my nose. Yes, I'd just had a good time with myself reading the werewolf story, but I miss Jalen terribly—the *real* Jalen, not the fantasy book equivalent.

I am really glad he's coming home. This latest two-week Zurich jaunt, by way of London, really was too much. I haven't even been in the same room with him for seventeen days. It's ridiculous.

I hope it's different from the last time he had to go to London. The last time, it was planned, but he got stuck at Heathrow for an extra five hours, he missed his connection at O'Hare, and he didn't get home until way after midnight.

His jet lag was horrible for almost a week; it was like living with a stranger.

"Maybe," I had purred, snuggling into him, "when you wake up at two a.m. and can't get back to sleep, you could wake me up, too, and we could do some fun things. Some naughty things."

"I'd like that, babe," he'd said, squeezing my hand and looking at me with sweet, dark brown eyes that couldn't hide how tired he was. He was fast asleep when I got upstairs, but I put on a red camisole before I got into bed, hoping he'd be encouraged that I wanted to get frisky when he woke up at two in the morning.

But when I woke up, it wasn't the middle of the night. Sunlight was streaming through the window. I blinked and rubbed my eyes, and Jalen wasn't next to me in bed. I got up, peed, washed my hands, and then went downstairs. A fresh pot of coffee was almost finished brewing. "Hey," I said, half curious but mostly annoyed. "Weren't you planning to wake me up last night?"

"I was," Jalen said, "but let's just say you made it clear that whatever you'd said at seven o'clock, your position on the matter had changed by two in the morning."

I tilted my head. "What?"

"Little bit of your elbow in my ribs."

My face fell. "Seriously? I hit you?"

"Well, it wasn't hard. Just enough to let me know that I shouldn't try it again."

"Goddammit. I was *so* in the mood when I went to bed."

"I'm sorry, babe. It's just this crazy travel schedule."

I'd hesitated but decided to press him. "I *miss* you, Jalen. I know it's only been a year, but this sucks. I miss you. I miss falling asleep in your arms. I miss your kisses. I miss making love to you."

Jalen nodded. "Yeah. I miss all of that too."

"And trying to get pregnant is already putting enough of a strain on decent sex. Between giving myself rectal exams to figure out when I'm ovulating, and you never being *home* when I *am* ovulating, we haven't exactly been on the same page."

"I know, but I'm home for two weeks now—"

"No," I corrected him, "you are home for *one* more week, and you have to leave on Sunday morning. *Again*. That's half the weekend."

"I have to be there in Zurich on Monday for the weekly meeting—"

"And you haven't even gotten over the jet lag yet. It's really like you're gone for three weeks a month instead of two."

He frowned and his eyes turned down. "I—"

I glared at him, and he stopped talking.

An uncomfortable silence fell between us for a few minutes until he shifted uncomfortably on the sofa.

"This isn't right," he said. "With me making a lot more money in this job, our lives were supposed to be better. But my life isn't better. I'm constantly exhausted. I don't even know what country I'm in half the time." He looked at me. "And you're not happy, either."

"We moved to Sacramento so we could start a family," I said, "and I can't do that when the dick I need is on another continent."

Jalen smiled sadly. "Sure, I get that."

"I'm *not* getting that," I'd said. "I'm not getting anything.

Maybe you can talk to Mariel or Roger. See if you can transfer."

Shock registered on his face. "Mariel took a chance on me to promote me. It hasn't even been a year yet. It's not like she's traveling any less than me. And *she's* got kids."

"I'm not saying it's not rough on her too. I'm just saying that I'm not happy."

"If you can just hang in there a little while longer—"

"I don't know that I *can* hang in there a little while longer."

The corners of his mouth turned down. "Okay, okay. Let me ask around a little bit. If there's someone who's itching to work the European markets, maybe that will work. Mariel will be disappointed, but if there's someone who can replace me and it can be an easy transition, then maybe I can make it happen."

"Or you can look for another job."

I remembered how Jalen looked at me out of the corner of his eye then, torn between an unhappy wife and a job he tolerated to get to where he wanted to go.

And, of course, Mariel is gone now.

Maybe the ex-girlfriend in his boss's job is just the kick in the ass Jalen needs to get out.

The water continues to cascade over my head, through my hair, falling loudly to the floor of the shower.

After I wash and condition my hair, I shave my body carefully. Not that Jalen is picky about my body hair. He's never mentioned it when my legs are stubbly, and he doesn't seem to prefer anything in particular with my pubic hair, whether it's a full bush or if I'm shaved completely. "Surprise me," he said with a smirk, when I asked him about it once.

I remember the first time I surprised Jalen—not with a creative shaving method or anything. It was with my presence.

It was back in November of our freshman year of college. I'd broken up with Ty about three weeks before. My roommate, Gina, with whom I shared a tiny dorm room at UC Irvine, had an older brother who was a junior at Arrowhead. Neither of us had class on Fridays that semester, so we left after class on Thursday, and we were on the Arrowhead campus by six o'clock.

"You're friends with the big basketball stud who goes here?" Gina asked as we got out of the car and carried our overnight bags to his apartment.

"I don't know if I'd call Jalen a *friend*. We went to high school together. I heard he had a thing for me, but he had a girlfriend. Then he broke up with her senior year, asked me out, and we went on a date."

"Oh, interesting."

"Not really. We were both too shy to talk to each other or something. Anyway, nothing happened except his ex-girlfriend got mad at me."

"How come nothing happened?"

"I'm not really sure. I know I was really nervous. He's really a beautiful specimen of masculinity."

"Well, look at *you*."

"Yes, I know, he's out of my league."

Gina looked me up and down. "No, that's not what I was going to say. I just know the type."

"The type?"

"The type of guy who likes the type of girl like you." She

started to head up the stairs to the second floor where her brother's apartment was.

I looked at Gina out of the corner of my eye. "A girl like me?"

She laughed. "Yeah, I know, it sounds weird. I guess you don't see it when you're in the middle of it."

"I guess I don't. Are you complimenting me or insulting me?"

"Neither. I'm just saying, there are a lot of guys who *definitely* have a type that looks pretty much exactly like you."

I was quiet as we walked down the second-floor corridor to her brother's apartment.

We got to his door and it opened. A tall white guy, with long curly black hair and Gina's soft dark eyes and button nose, stood in the doorway.

"Asswipe!"

"Skankface!" He pulled her into a big bear hug and lifted her off the ground. "Great to see you, baby sis!"

She hopped out of his grasp. "Rachel, Tony. Tony, Rachel. Tony makes the best margaritas."

He grabbed Gina's bag. "Come on in. Just set your stuff in the living room. You can use the pull-out couch, or we've got an air mattress in the closet." I had my sleeping bag in the trunk of Gina's car, so that was fine.

"Tony, did you know that Rachel *dated* Jalen Jefferson?"

I rolled my eyes. "Gina, that is *not* a big deal. It was one date."

"Well, she still went to high school with him."

Tony nodded, looking impressed. "Well, the party we want to get into tonight is supposedly the same one where Jalen will be . It's one of the big houses near Greek Row, but it's not Greek. They've got one of the local bands playing, too. It's gonna be great. You been to parties in Irvine?"

"Uh... sure." I had, but they were pretty lame. Irvine was more of a commuter school and there were a lot of engineering geeks there. I mean, I was one of them, but still.

"Come on," Tony said. "I'll take you two to dinner."

Dinner was a burrito from a hole-in-the-wall taqueria where they didn't speak English. Tony conversed with the cashier for several minutes in Spanish before he walked back over to us. "You aren't vegetarian, are you, Rachel?"

"No." My eyes narrowed. "You didn't order me anything weird, did you?"

He turned to Gina. "Is she always this suspicious of everyone?"

Gina shrugged. "You get used to it."

We got back to Tony's apartment and he made us a batch of frozen margaritas to preparty. I drank the first one a little too fast and got a brain freeze headache. Tony's friend Michael showed up at the door right as I was pouring the last bits of tequila and ice down the back of my throat. Tony introduced us, and Michael started flirting with Gina. Tony narrowed his eyes at his friend, who didn't get the hint.

I poured myself a second margarita, and Tony, ever the protective big brother, told me to watch it since we hadn't actually gone out to start drinking yet. I dismissed him with my hand. "I'm not a little ninety-pound weakling like Gina," I said, who was on her third. "I got a big ass to soak up all this alcohol."

He nodded warily. I already sounded a little tipsy.

I drank the second margarita more slowly as Gina and Michael made eyes at each other and Tony got more surly. I wondered if Tony would go for me if Gina weren't around—or if Gina weren't being hit on so hard by his friend.

As I went into the kitchen to grab more pretzels, Tony pulled Michael to the side, near the stairs off the living room, and spoke in a low voice to him. I walked back to the living room and sat next to Gina on the sofa, right where Michael had been sitting.

"Hey," Gina said, slurring her words. "That was the place that the boy Michael was sitting and I liked him sitting there."

I patted her knee. "Right, babe. And now I'll sit here for a minute while Michael and Tony have a little talk."

Gina sat forward and looked in my eyes, seriously, but a little unsteadily. "Tony is a good brother, okay, I know that, Rachel, he totally is. But he still sees me as a little girl, you know what I mean?"

"Yeah."

"See, Rachel," Gina said unsteadily, "*you* get me. You know what I'm going through."

"Do you *like* Michael?"

"Well, I mean, he's cute and all. He's got a pretty good ass. But it's just the *idea* of it all, you know?" She asked the last part a little too loudly and then her voice dropped to a whisper. "I mean, it's not like Tony has a bad opinion of Michael. He probably wants me to be a nun or something."

"Smash the goddamn patriarchy," I agreed.

"I mean, if I want to fuck Michael tonight, I'll fuck Michael tonight, and there's nothing Tony can do about it."

"Volume, sweetie," I said, patting her hand.

She raised her voice even more. "I'll be as loud as I want to be."

"Okay, but just, hold on for a second. How would *you* react if *I* were flirting with Tony?"

"Oh my God," she said. "Do you like Tony? His last girlfriend was *such* a bitch. He did everything for her and—"

"No, no, no, that's not my point," I said. Then I sighed. "Never mind. You go do what you want. Go suck Michael's dick, or whatever you think will piss your brother off the most."

Tony went into the kitchen and Michael walked back to the sofa. He looked at me and tilted his head. I looked up at him. He clearly didn't appreciate me cock-blocking him, and even though Gina wasn't giving him play for the right reasons, it wasn't really up to me to stand in their way. Or *sit* in their way, as the case may be.

I patted Gina's knee. "Remember to use a condom."

Gina crinkled her nose at me. "Got a twelve-pack in my purse."

"Ever the optimist," I said, getting up.

I wandered into the kitchen where Tony was rummaging through the fridge. "Sorry," I said. "I tried."

"I don't know why I treat her like she's my responsibility to protect," Tony mumbled, mostly to himself. "Since I'm meeting Monica at the party, I guess he wanted some female companionship tonight."

"Monica?"

"My girlfriend. Gina didn't tell you?"

"She said you broke up with someone."

"Yeah, like at the beginning of the summer." He closed the kitchen door and wandered over to the table. "Monica and I have been dating for a couple of months." He had a clear view into the living room, and glanced over at Michael and Gina on the sofa, flirting and laughing. "Jeez, why did he have to go for my sister?"

I shrugged. "Some guys like the trim, athletic type. Other guys like curvy girls. I can tell Michael's the former." My thoughts went straight to Jalen, watching me in the halls, Alicia on his arm but not in his head. "It is what it is."

"Sorry. I didn't mean for it to sound like I was trying to set you up with my douchebag friend."

I leaned against the wall of the kitchen and crossed my arms. "Honestly, I'm just glad *someone* is trying to get me laid."

Tony laughed and then looked at his watch. "All right, I guess those two can separate long enough to walk to the party."

"It's walking distance?"

"About a half mile. Parking sucks down there, and none of us are going be sober enough to drive home anyway. You ready to go?"

"I actually wanted to change before we left."

Tony frowned. "Tell me this won't be one of those 'I'll just be ten minutes' and then it takes forty-five minutes and my bathroom looks like the makeup counter at the mall exploded."

It's my turn to laugh. "No. I mean, probably not. I'll throw on a dress and touch up my makeup."

I went upstairs to the bathroom with my overnight bag, and I pulled out a dress. I'd pictured showing up to the party and Jalen seeing me from across the room. I don't really know what I expected next. I'd already blown it on my date with him, but perhaps if I showed myself to my fullest advantage, he'd come over to talk to me. There were no halls in which to see each other on Monday. No jealous ex-girl-friends with perfect tits to scowl at me from across Spanish class, no rumor mill, no people mumbling my name in the halls talking about my huge tits or my big ass. Maybe without any of those distractions, I'd actually have the guts to talk to him. To have a real conversation. The worst that could happen was that I'd make a fool of myself and Gina and I would drive an hour and a half home and I'd never set foot on the Arrowhead campus—and never see Jalen Jefferson—ever again.

I pulled my sweatshirt, jeans, and T-shirt off, and then took my comfortable but ugly bra and panties off too. I stood in the bathroom naked and looked at my reflection, taking deep breaths, trying to convince myself that this, the womanly curvaceous form in the mirror was exactly what Jalen wanted.

Lots of things could have changed. Maybe he had a girl-friend, maybe he was such a stud on the basketball team that the sophisticated cheerleaders and rich girls were throwing themselves at him. But I looked in the mirror. I hadn't changed much in the six months since Jalen had last seen me in the corridors of Montrose High School, trying not to stare at me hungrily, like he wanted to take me right there, but utterly failing.

I put on a flattering red bra, lacy and pretty, a near-impossible task to find with a body like mine. The brassiere gods had smiled upon me that day in the lingerie store in the Irvine Spectrum. I fished out the matching thong panties from my bag. I'd never worn these beyond trying them on in the dorm room when Gina was gone. I'd debated with myself over wearing them, but the thong made my ass look sexy and gave me a little confidence. I knew that there was very little chance of any scenario happening in which Jalen would see me in the thong in all its glory, but hey, when else would I wear it? The least I could do for myself was try to look as sexy as possible. If it didn't work on Jalen, I'd still be sensual and confident. Who knows what might happen at a house party on Greek Row on a Friday night?

I stepped into the dress and shimmied it up over my hips and then pulled it up to my armpits, tucking my breasts into the front. I put my arms in the sleeves, Reaching behind myself, I zipped up the back. I exhaled and lifted my eyes to look at myself in the mirror.

I had obviously forgotten how sexy I looked in the dress. It was perfect. It hugged all the curves it should accentuate, and minimized all the curves I wanted it to minimize. I tried to ignore how much the dress had cost because it was absolutely perfect.

With its cap sleeves and flouncy skirt, with its tight accentuating bodice and its narrow waist, the dress was fun and flirty but fairly conservative in its coverage. It didn't look that conservative on me, though, because everything about it showed off my curves.

I touched up my makeup, not really doing much more than I'd done for the daytime, packed everything up in my overnight bag, and walked back downstairs. Michael, Tony, and Gina were sitting on the sofa talking and all three of them did a double-take when I walked in. It was almost cartoonish.

"Holy shit, Rachel," Gina said. "You look amazing. If I had a dick, I would *totally* want to fuck you."

"Uh, thanks, creepy girl," I said. "I wanted to look nice for the party tonight."

"Wait a second," Gina said. "It's because *Jalen* will be there, isn't it? Is that the only reason you agreed to drive down with me?"

"No, no," I said, blushing. "I wanted to meet your brother and see the campus."

Gina laughed. "Oh my God. You must *really* want a do-over on that date."

"It wasn't that big of a deal."

"Uh, yeah, I don't believe you. Not when you see him for the first time since graduation wearing a dress like *that*."

I was mortified, but I cleared my throat and acted impatient. I tapped my foot, still in my sneakers. "So will we stay here and make fun of the fact that there's a hot guy I want to screw at this party, or are we *actually* going to the party?"

Michael and Gina looked at each other and then both looked at Tony. "Yeah, sure," Gina said. "We'll go to the party." But the tone of her voice suggested that she just wanted to stay in Tony's apartment and make out with Michael. Or maybe find some excuse to go over to Michael's apartment and ditch her judgmental brother altogether.

"Anyone up for a tequila shot before we hit the road?" Michael asked, getting up from the sofa and walking into the kitchen. He came back with two full shot glasses, salt, and two wedges of lime.

"Hell no," Gina said. "I did straight tequila shots *once*. I'm not doing that again."

Looking at everyone else in the room, I realized I was overdressed. *Really* overdressed. Everyone else was in jeans and T-shirts and sweatshirts, and I was in a dress that was almost fancy enough—and slutty enough—to go clubbing. I was so interested in turning Jalen's head when I entered the room that I had totally forgotten other people existed—people I had to interact with, people who'd have opinions of me.

Maybe I should go change.

But picturing the look in Jalen's eyes when he'd see me, his curvy muse, wearing the only hot red dress in a sea of denim and cotton T-shirts—

Fuck it. I just needed some liquid courage. I stepped to Michael and took a shot out of his hand. "I'll drink it if Gina doesn't want it." I downed the alcohol without the salt beforehand or the lime afterward, pouring it directly in my mouth so I wouldn't mess up my lipstick.

I swallowed, feeling the tequila burn all the way down. "All right, guys," I said. "Let's get going." I looked at Tony. "You said Monica was meeting us there?"

He nodded.

Tony grabbed his backpack, and I kicked my sneakers off and put my heels on.

"Whoa," Tony said. "We've got a fifteen-minute walk. You're seriously walking a half-miles in those heels?"

I shrugged. "I'll be okay."

"I'm not carrying your drunk ass home," Gina slurred.

Tony and I walked ahead of Michael and Gina, and Tony was untalkative and brusque, kicking at the ground all the way to the party, his displeasure heightening the closer Michael and Gina got to each other and the farther away they got from us. My shoes started to hurt my feet after about ten minutes, but I didn't say anything.

When we turned the corner to the street where the party

was, we found ourselves at a large house surrounded by a fence with a high gate. He brightened as a young woman in a tank top and tight jeans with artfully placed rips in the thighs and knees bounded across the front yard of the party house and jumped into his arms, kissing him.

I started to leave the two of them there at the gate, but the girlfriend broke from the kiss, and looked at me out of the corner of her eye, not just at my face, but up and down, appraising my slutty dress and heels.

"So who's this, Tony?"

"My kid sister's friend Rachel. She came down from Irvine. I guess she went to school with Jalen Jefferson."

She looked at me and nodded. "And you might see Jalen tonight."

I shrugged, trying to be noncommittal, but my dress had committed for me. "I guess. I'll get out of your hair." I opened the gate. "See you guys in there."

The party was in full swing. The lights in the house burned brightly, and I could see how crowded it was. There seemed to be people packed in everywhere, in every room, in every hall.

The band was on a makeshift stage in the large front room, their backs to the wall separating the room from the kitchen. Fluorescent light from the kitchen leaked into the large room, messing up the mood a little. But they were loud and played a fun dance song from the eighties that they were putting their own spin on. I recognized the song but couldn't quite place it. People were dancing inside the house, outside the house, everywhere. I wish I'd had someone to dance with. Everyone else at the party was wearing Arrowhead sweatshirts, jeans, and casual shoes. There were a couple of skinny girls in summery dresses inside, where it was probably a lot warmer than outside. I strained to see through the windows, but there was no sign of Jalen anywhere.

I looked at the ground. The pathway was concrete and went all the way to the door, but there was grass on either side, and that's where people were dancing. Not good for heels.

I decided to try my luck to find Jalen inside. I walked down the pathway toward the house, and as I did, the porch light illuminated me. Several heads turned, a few just because of the changing light, but then a few more because of my slutty dress, my boobs spilling out the top, the too-short hem threatening to expose my ass. I took a deep breath and kept walking.

Oof. The tequila started to hit me, but it didn't affect my balance. Not much, anyway. I walked up the two steps to the porch and opened the door to the house.

Just then, the band broke out into "Red Skies at Night" and the cheap stage lights flickered over to red. Had I not been wearing a dress and heels that made me so self-conscious, that made me look like an actual call girl, it'd be cool to come to a party where the band actually brought its own light system. But I was only aware of trying to put one foot in front of the other without falling over and embarrassing myself even more that I already had.

"Hey, girl," a voice said in my ear. I turned and it was a tall white guy with a plaid flannel shirt on over camouflage pants with rips in both knees. "You look like you came to party." I feel his eyes all over me.

"I came here to see Jalen," I said back to him.

He grinned. "So does everyone. Don't worry about it—

he's somewhere in the house. I haven't seen him since he arrived." He puts his hand around my back and I tried not to let the cringe show on my face. "I haven't seen you around here before. You a freshman?"

"Uh," I said, "I'm actually visiting from another school."

"Oh, I gotcha," he said. "They must throw classier parties than we do."

I gave him my best confused glare.

"Because you're dressed like a fuckin' boss bitch," he said, laughing. "Here, when we go to nice parties, it means our beer T-shirts don't have any stains on them. You're probably insulted we didn't have a red carpet and Joan Rivers interviewing you before you walked in."

I turned my face to him with a tight smile and tried to spin out of his arms.

"Whoa," he said. "Don't leave just yet. I can probably find Jalen for you."

"Oh," I said, unsure. "Do you know where he might be?"

"Sure, everyone tries to get close to him, especially after that damn b-ball master class he gave a few weeks ago on national TV."

I weighed my options. "Oh, I get it. Well, I'm a friend from high school."

The guy nodded. "All right, not just a groupie then."

"Uh—no. Does he really have groupies?"

"It'll die down. They'll lose a few games, Jalen will stop putting up triple-doubles, no one will even remember who he is." He stepped toward me conspiratorially and lowered his voice. "Probably better for him anyway. He's not cut out for the limelight, if you ask me."

Oh, for fuck's sake. Jalen was a goddamn celebrity at this

school. He basically had bouncers running interference for him. By the looks of it, they got to hit on all the girls who were trying to get close to Jalen. And basketball season was in full bloom anyway; Jalen wouldn't have any time for anything but practice, games, and schoolwork. This had been such a bad idea. No wonder I'd kept my agenda hidden from Gina. I hadn't even believed in it myself.

"Oh, okay," I said, breathing out. "I tell you what. If he doesn't want to see anyone tonight, I don't want to bother him. Maybe you can get a message to him."

The white bouncer dude seemed a little taken aback by my response. "Uh, I don't know. I'm no secretary."

If I could get a message to Jalen, maybe he would at least give me a phone call over the weekend. We had another forty hours here before we had to leave on Sunday afternoon.

Did I want to use my sexuality on this bouncer douchebag just to get the message to Jalen?

Yeah, I decided I did.

I leaned forward just a bit and shook my boobs very subtly. I could have been accused of not even being aware I'd done it. "Are you sure? It would really mean a lot to me."

He didn't even try to pretend he wasn't looking at my tits. "Yeah, okay. What's the message?"

"Tell him that Rachel from high school is visiting this weekend. He should still have my cell number."

"Yeah, okay."

"Thanks." I turned out of his grasp and walked back toward the front door. I could feel the bouncer douchebag's eyes watch me—probably my ass, but maybe also my sneakily sexy calves—and then I was out the door.

My legs almost gave out on the porch. I wasn't sure what I was doing, coming down to Arrowhead for the weekend. Not only was the boy I came down to see not even *remotely* close to available, but my roommate was getting her groove on with her brother's friend, which definitely made for the promise of an extremely awkward weekend. I just pictured Gina spending the night at Michael's, and Tony having to deal with his kid sister's friend in the slutty red dress while his new girlfriend kept giving me the stink eye. I was looking at forty hours of hell.

I wondered if someone could drop me off at the Mojave Sunset station. I could have taken the late train back to Irvine, where I might have been able to salvage part of the weekend.

There was a bench on the front porch, made of dark wood and wrought iron. It seemed a little nice for a party house. Miraculously, no one was sitting on it, so I stepped over to it and took a load off. My feet immediately started to hurt. It had only been thirty minutes in those heels and while they were very sexy, I was about dead. And in a party this crowded, no one could see my shoes, anyway.

I hadn't even gone over to the keg to fill up a red Solo cup with cheap beer. I scanned the grass area. I didn't see any of the people I came with. I wondered if I'd ever see Gina again. Maybe she and Michael would drive to Vegas in the morning, get married, and work in the casinos for the rest of their lives.

Two guys, one white and one Asian, both in Arrowhead sweatshirts, came stumbling up the steps, laughing. The white one looked at me and said, "Holy fuck, those are some *nice* tits." The Asian guy pulled him back and they both went inside.

What am I even doing here?

The door opened and a tall black guy stepped out onto the porch. He looked familiar, but I couldn't see him very well. He had on a hoodie, low over his face, and he looked across the yard, as if he was searching for something.

I could only see his back from my angle. But his jeans were tight on him, and that sweet ass looked the same as it had in the Montrose High hallway the day he'd asked me out.

It was him.

"Jalen," I called.

He spun around and saw me sitting on the bench. I stood, partially because he was standing, but mostly because I wanted him to see me in this sexy dress with the stiletto heels.

He smiled. "Rachel," he said, "I was hoping I'd find you."

PREEMPTIVE STRIKE

Jalen and I went inside. The bouncer douchebag who'd tried to hit on me let us past a gate across the stairs and we went up. Jalen led the way into a room along the hall, and I followed him.

The room was dimly lit by low-wattage bulbs beneath heavy beige shades on identical, black wrought-iron lamps that sat in the two back corners of the room. I looked around. All the walls as well as the ceiling were painted a dark blue that looked almost black. Iridescent stars, mostly small, were glued to the ceiling and the upper walls.

"Interesting," I said. "Like the night sky."

"It's cool, isn't it? I wish my dorm room was like this."

"This isn't your room?"

"No, my brother's friend is spending the semester in Italy. He's letting me stay here until he gets back." He opened up a minifridge under the desk. "You want a beer? I've got a nice juice mix, too, one of those strawberry-kiwi-mandarin things. I can throw some rum in it if you want."

"Sure, that sounds good."

He grabbed a couple of tumblers off the desk and poured juice, with a generous amount of spiced rum, in each.

"Sorry," he said, "I don't have an icemaker."

"You're throwing a party and you're not even down there celebrating with your friends?" I took the glass from him and we both sat on the bed.

"Not really my scene."

I looked back up at the ceiling. Jalen's brother's friend had actually put up some constellations. I recognized one.

"Is that Ursa Minor?" I asked, pointing.

"Probably. Felix is an astronomy major. This whole room is probably accurate to a crazy degree."

"How come you're staying here instead of in the dorms?"

"Well, technically I *am* staying in the dorms," he said. "All freshmen have to live on campus. But after the Nevada game, I couldn't get any peace in my dorm. People dropping by at all hours of the night. I couldn't get any sleep. It's been crazy. I can't answer my phone. Reporters are camped out on the lawn at my parents' house, girls calling me at three in the morning, people stealing my clothes when I'm in the shared shower in the dorm."

"Stealing your clothes?"

He smiled. "Yeah. It's nuts. I lost my Tiger Lily Serenade concert tee." He tilted his head. "So, why did you come here?"

"I, uh, I guess I wanted...." I said, and then I stopped talking.

"You guess you wanted what?"

My chest tightened again and I quickly took a drink. It was strong, but it was also really tasty, and I drank a little more quickly than I was expecting to.

"Spit it out, Rachel."

"Spit out the drink?"

He rolled his eyes. "No, girl, spit out the thing you were about to say."

I looked at the ceiling, wondering if I could find Orion's Belt, or Sirius, the Dog Star. Words failed me. I didn't know how the truth would sound. I took a deep breath and decided to plunge ahead.

"I like you a lot, Jalen. I really wanted our date to work."

"Our date—last year?"

I grimaced. I knew he hadn't been obsessing about what could have gone better that night like I had, but to hear him mention our date made me cringe a little. I didn't see how to get out of the conversation gracefully.

"Yeah. I mean, I really wanted to go out with you. But then everyone at school was talking about it."

Jalen nodded. "I know. And then it was this *huge* deal, right?"

"Right."

I paused. "I guess I built it up a lot in my head, and then when we actually *went* on the date, I just clammed up."

He didn't say anything.

"I was kind of hoping you'd give me another chance, but a couple of weeks later, you were back with Alicia." I looked at his face, but couldn't read his expression. Maybe he was confused, or maybe he was just taking it all in. I didn't see any shock or disgust, so I barreled on, examining my hand so I wouldn't have to watch his face anymore. "I was flipping channels a few weeks ago when I saw you on television."

"The Nevada game?"

"That was it," I said. "You scored a lot of points. The

PREEMPTIVE STRIKE | 151

announcer said it was some sort of school record. And, oh man, this'll sound really stupid, but I was still just as attracted to you as I was in high school." I glanced quickly at his face and then back down again. "I was even dating someone else at the time. I had no idea that you were the star of the team. Aren't you a freshman? Don't seniors usually become the stars?"

"Not so much in basketball. It's complicated."

"Okay." I cleared my throat. "Anyway, I felt this—this need to see you again. I know you were attracted to me in high school, and I thought maybe if I came down here and we could hang out for a while, you'd want to go out with me again."

There was no way I could look at Jalen because I was terrified of his reaction. Had his attraction to me down-graded into friendship, or worse—nothing?

I heard him exhale loudly. *Oh no.* I braced myself.

"Oh God," he said. "I'm such a fucking idiot."

"You're what?" I turned to him, my heart leaping.

And then he was kissing me.

The kiss surprised me at first, and then I relaxed into it. He took my face in his hands, so gentle, and then after a moment he pulled back.

"I—" He gasped. "I'm sorry. I *had* to kiss you. Especially after you said that."

"Goddammit," I said. "If I'd only been—"

"No." Jalen's voice was firm. "I was even more nervous than you were. You're *so* beautiful. I'm *so* attracted to you. I've never *stopped* being attracted to you. So much that some-times it's physically uncomfortable."

"Well, if you just adjust your underwear—"

"Not like that," he said softly, grinning. "Like, my heart is uncomfortable. It hurts to see you and not be with you."

"Oh," I said.

"I totally fucked up that night," Jalen said. "My friend Eric, he used to watch the two of us look at each other in the hall, and just shake his head. He's the one who finally convinced me to break up with Alicia and ask you out."

"He—he what?"

"He could see how hot we were for each other. He used to say that when we looked at each other it was rated MA."

Ha. Sounds like Elaine. "Well, then, why did we just stare at each other all evening and not talk?"

"Eric had a theory about that. He said we were *too* attracted to each other. He said we needed to, uh—you know what, never mind."

"No, no, really, what?"

"I shouldn't mention it. It was nothing."

"Well, now," I said, putting my hand on his arm. "You really have to tell me."

He laughed nervously and then took a drink of the rum and juice. I sipped my boozy punch too.

"Okay. He said before we could go on another date, we just had to have raw, passionate animal sex. Get it all out of our system so it wouldn't be in the way when we finally went on the date."

I laughed. "We were both unbelievably tense."

"Yeah."

I took another drink, and even though we were talking seriously about both wanting to have sex with each other, I could feel myself starting to loosen up, the nervousness I always felt around him falling away. "You know, it's funny."

"What?"

"My friend Elaine said the same thing."

"Really? That we were so nervous around each other we just needed to have sex to get it out of our system?"

"Pretty much her exact words. I wonder if she and Eric discussed this theory before they told us."

"Maybe." Jalen smiled.

"Notice we're talking now, like, a real conversation. Thanks to Elaine and Eric."

He raised his glass. "And to my friend Captain Morgan."

I clinked our glasses together. "We don't really need the alcohol to have a real conversation, do we? I mean, I always figured you and I would be really good together."

"So did I," he said. "I was just an idiot."

"No," I said firmly. "You weren't an idiot. Maybe it was, I don't know, inflated expectations. Like, there was so much about what everyone at school wanted our date to be, and neither one of us had any idea how to live up to all of it. Those expectations killed our relationship before it even started."

"Maybe." Jalen paused. "Or maybe we needed to start somewhere different. Somewhere we could be free from our parents' curfews and stuff like that."

"Somewhere like college?"

"Right."

"No, that's not it. My dad loved you, by the way. You're probably the only guy who's taken me on a date that he didn't complain about."

He laughed. "That's good to know." He looked out of the corner of his eye at me. "That would be kind of unusual, you know."

"It would?"

"Yeah. Alicia's parents *hated* me. I've dated a couple other white girls, too. Their parents weren't thrilled when I showed up on their front door to pick up their daughter."

I shrugged. "I've dated a few other guys, too. You were the only one who got me flowers, and you're one of the few who came in and introduced yourself to my father."

We sat in silence for a moment. "Do you believe," I said carefully, "what Eric and Elaine said?"

"What, that when we look at each other it's like an NC-17 movie? Maybe. I know Alicia noticed it. We fought about it a lot, and I apologized over and over. That's why we broke up. Both times."

"Not about the hot looks we gave each other in the hall-ways at school," I said, shaking my head. "About us needing to get sex out of the way before we can go on a decent date."

Jalen's mouth opened and then closed. "I don't know. He might have a point, I guess. Neither of us could even talk."

"Yeah. It was definitely weird."

"Of course, that's not really how I was raised. I mean, I didn't wait for marriage or anything, but I'm also not a one-night-stand kind of guy."

"This wouldn't be a one-night stand," I said. He jerked his head up, just slightly, but I noticed. Oh, I didn't put that in past tense. *This* wouldn't be a one-night stand. Not *that* wouldn't have been a one-night stand. I just told him I wanted to sleep with him tonight. I studied his face, but, to my surprise, it didn't look like I'd fazed him. We'd kissed. We'd never done that before.

I touched his arm again. His body was solid and substantial, like he knew what he wanted and he knew how to get it.

I could show him that I could be bold too. I took a deep breath and plowed forward. "Having sex with you tonight would be a simple acknowledgment that our relationship will have to start differently from the other ones you've had." I nodded, as if I was trying to convince myself. "And that goes for me, too. I've never slept with someone on the first date, and I've certainly never slept with someone *before* the first date."

"We've already had a first date."

I looked out of the corner of my eye at him. "Over a year ago."

"Still inside the statute of limitations, if you ask me." Jalen raised his eyebrows. "Are you suggesting this is a very real possibility?"

"I don't know," I said, biting my lip and looking up at him.

Then the nerves come back. I'd just hit the ball into his court. And for what? Why did I do that? I could be in my dorm room in Irvine tomorrow if I wanted, never to see Jalen again. What the hell was I playing at?

"No, Jalen, that's not true. I absolutely know. Yes, I'm suggesting it. I want to have sex with you. I've wanted to have sex with you since the day you asked me out. Probably even before. I'm very attracted to you. I know you're very attracted to me, too. As stupid as it is to drive eighty miles for a boy, I wore these stripper heels and this slutty dress here just to get you to notice me."

"You didn't need the dress," Jalen said sheepishly. "As soon as Tim told me 'Rachel's here,' I literally ran downstairs. I've been kicking myself for striking out with you on our date." He hesitated. "Look, I don't *want* this to be a one-night stand. Do you go to school around here?"

"UC Irvine."

"Oh, right. You said eighty miles." He paused. "So this would be long distance."

Even though it was making me nervous that he and I, in his head, were already in a relationship after two kisses and a bad date a year ago, I couldn't deny that I was thinking about it also.

Stranger things had happened. Would staying the night here in Jalen's borrowed room change anything? Yes. It might mean we'd go on a real date tomorrow. And if that date went well, we might end up in bed again. And then maybe again the next day. Hell, I would have been okay spending the whole weekend in bed with Jalen and just pulling myself out from between the sheets to eat.

"We don't have to put any pressure on it." I encircled his wrist with my fingers and lifted his hand away from his body, placing it on my chest, above my breasts. I could feel his fingers lightly caress my collarbone. His whole hand raised and lowered with my chest as I inhaled and exhaled. I closed my eyes and breathed deeply, trying to calm myself, but I caught Jalen's scent.

He still wore the same cologne as he had high school, a rich, heady mixture of grapefruit and cinnamon and new leather. I wondered how my perfume smelled to him. I changed when I started college—new school, new life, new perfume. I didn't really like it, though, and after I broke up with Ty, I went back to the scent I wore my senior year, a mixture of rose and something the box says is heliotrope, whatever that is.

I wanted Jalen to be close enough to me to breathe in my perfume, to flash him back to the halls of our school, where he couldn't ever drink enough of me in with his eyes. If I had only known senior year what I knew now. I would have made the first move. I would have leaned over on the way to dinner and kissed him. I would have straddled him in the driver's seat, aching for him to get inside my panties, undoing his belt desperately. Jalen and I needed the physical release with each other back then, and sitting on the bed next to him, his hand on my chest, we both needed it tonight as well.

I tried to keep my breathing steady, but his hand shook.

"We're both nervous now that it seems like this might actually happen," I whispered. "Goddamn it, Jalen, if we don't fuck each other's brains out, we'll end up frustrated and horny at the end of the night—again."

He leaned forward and kissed me once more, and I didn't even pretend I could control my emotions this time. I kissed him back, opening my mouth and inviting his tongue in. He broke from the kiss just long enough to say, "Oh my God, Rachel, you are *so* beautiful," and I knew that he would love every angle and curve of my body, even the parts that I'd never liked. I reached for his fly and got the top button open, and he moved his hand to the zipper at the back of my dress, desperate to remove my clothes.

I stopped kissing him and stood up, my breasts spilling out the top of the dress, my hair in my eyes, my heels still on. I briefly considered kicking off the heels, but keeping them on felt sexier, especially for the first time with Jalen. He looked up at me from his seated position on the bed, and his eyes were tender, yet belied a fervent desire that I could sense. The heat intensified between my legs. I unzipped the back of the dress and shimmied and shook until it slid down over my hips. I stepped out of the dress and then tossed it over the desk chair. I stood in front of Jalen in a cute, sexy bra and the thong I hadn't been sure I should wear and my heels and nothing else.

He watched me for a moment as the band downstairs started a slow, sensual song—bands didn't normally play slow songs at parties like this, but hey, everyone was drunk or stoned. Maybe people were starting to couple up. I had to stop my brain from obsessing about the logistics of the band song and concentrate on grinding my body in time to the music.

I swiveled my hips first, and he moved his gaze to travel up my body, locking eyes with me.

"Are you ready for this?" I whispered.

"I'm been waiting for this for *years*," he said.

I stepped closer to him, and I reached down and took his hands and placed them firmly just above the sides of my thong, where my waist flared out to my hips. I tried to ignore how much I disliked my soft belly, uncovered right in front of Jalen's face, but judging by the dazed look in his eyes, he didn't share my negative opinion. His hands were still shaking, though, just slightly.

"Damn," he said, barely audible under his breath and the din of the music and the dancing downstairs. I glanced down at him and bit my lip. It was the closest I'd ever been to him, the most exposed I'd ever been, and I couldn't wait for what would happen next.

He stood up from the bed, his hands still resting on my hips, and he kicked his shoes off. He leaned into me and kissed me again, this time with an open mouth from the very beginning, and his right hand moved around my back, embracing me firmly.

He removed his left hand from my right hip, and he unzipped his fly the rest of the way, letting his pants fall around his ankles. He pressed me closer to him, and I felt his erection through his boxers against the lower part of my stomach. I gasped. I expected to touch him, of course, but the *realness* of this moment, the fact that it was actually here, that I hadn't fucked anything up—it shocked me.

"Holy shit, Rachel," Jalen said, running his hands all over me, slowly, deliciously, while I breathed him in, his cock hard and urgent, separated from my skin by only a thin layer of cotton. I ran my hands from his shoulders, down his chest, over his T-shirt, and I stopped at the bottom hem at the same time as his hand stopped at my ass. He gave me a slow, light but sensual squeeze, and he moaned very softly, as if he was trying to hide how much I turned him on.

God, I'd never wanted anyone this much.

I pulled his shirt up and over his head, and his hands came off my body to make it easier for me to undress him. I gazed at his naked torso for the first time. I'd seen how strong he was, how big his biceps were, and noticed how his chest muscles were tight under his shirt. But I'd never seen him completely uncovered from the waist up, with just his boxers on.

"You're pretty hot, too, you know," I said to Jalen, running my eyes from his pecs to his abs to his erection, barely contained by his boxers. "Maybe you never caught me staring at you in the halls the way I caught you staring at me, but yeah, you're a very attractive man."

Jalen smiled coyly, and put a finger underneath my chin, raising my head and staring in my eyes. "You sure you want this?"

I nodded. "I've never wanted anyone to fuck me more than I want you to right now."

"I'll get a condom."

"Good."

He turned from me and his tight ass was right in front of me, tempting me to be naughty. I stepped forward as he opened the bedside table drawer. I ran my fingers around his waist and then underneath the waistband of his boxers. I began to lower them, inch by inch, as he found the box of condoms, pulled one out, and held the wrapped prophylactic in his hand. The resistance I felt in his boxers gave way when his erect penis was finally freed from the waistband, and he breathed in sharply.

I snaked my hand around to his front and wrapped it around his shaft, gently at first, and then with just a little more pressure.

"Oh, Rachel," he said gruffly, "don't you dare stop."

"I'm not planning on it," I whispered to him. "Not until you're ready to be inside me."

"Fuck, Rachel, I've been ready for so long."

"Maybe just a couple more strokes, big man. What do you say?"

"That would be fine," he said. And then he drew out the word *fine* as I gave him a strong, slow stroke, out and back, and he tilted his head and closed his eyes. "Oh, Rachel, that's *so* fine."

I pushed one string of thong down below my right hip, then moved my hand to the other side.

"I'm ready for you, Jalen," I said.

He tore the condom wrapper open, and as I continued to stroke him with my hand, he positioned the condom at the tip of his penis. I kissed his shoulder as I worked my thong down to my knees, removing my hand. He rolled the condom on his cock, and the moment seemed to hang in the air between us, that meant we would really be doing this.

The thong fell to my ankles. I stepped out of it, being careful not to catch it on the bottom of my high heels. I reached behind me and unhooked my bra as Jalen turned around.

"Oh," he said, "you took off your panties." He hooked his thumbs under the shoulder straps of my bra, and I held my arms out in front of me, letting him pull the bra off. I kept telling myself he loved my curves and his eyes were on my big tits as the bra cups uncovered them. Jalen was seeing me for the first time too, and finally seeing me the way he'd been waiting to for so long.

Am I as pretty as Alicia? I almost said, but I bit my tongue. Because I knew, intellectually if not exactly emotionally, that he considered me to be *more* beautiful than Alicia. I also knew that I didn't believe him, and part of me wanted to argue with him that he was crazy to want to have sex with a snarky, curvy, purple-haired girl like me when he could have a magazine cover model like her. But of course it would have been crazy to even bring Alicia's name up when he was naked in front of me, his cock so hard and wrapped up like a present for me to receive. I didn't want him to think of Alicia. I didn't want *myself* to think of Alicia. I just wanted him. I wanted him to have sex with me, to let the two of us get that palpable tension between us to end so that we could have a real conversation.

He looked into my face. "Is everything okay? Are you having second thoughts about this?"

"No," I said quickly. "I just—oh fuck, Jalen, you're so *cut*. And so smart, and so talented, and you were dating the—you could honestly have pretty much any woman you want."

"I'm glad to hear that I can have any woman I want," Jalen said, "because I want *you*, Rachel. I've wanted you for a long time. I fucked up our date, and I don't intend to fuck this up." He leaned back. "Are you sure you want this?"

"I definitely want this." I nodded vigorously. "I am *so* wet."

"Oh," he said, perhaps not expecting me to use that term. "Well, we'll have to take care of that, won't we?"

I was being silly and insecure, I knew. I was about to blow it.

Then I remembered what Elaine had told me when I ran for student council president.

"Just pretend like you're qualified and that you're the best candidate for the job."
"But I'm not."
"But you have to pretend you are."
"When do I stop pretending?"
Elaine shook her head. "You don't."

"Lie on your back," I said, hoping the edge to my voice would come out.

"What?"

"You heard me. Lie on your back."

Jalen gave me a lopsided smile.

"What are you waiting for?" I said, putting my hands on my hips. "A written invitation? My calligraphy's not that good."

He pulled the covers back, the clean flat sheet over the mattress. His erection still impossibly hard in front of him, he lay back, swinging his feet up. His cock, which had been almost parallel with the floor when he stood, was now at an upward angle. I noticed, too, that there was a slight curve to it, and a thrill ran up my back. *That cock has a lot of potential.*

I turned to him and put my right knee next to his right hip. He ran his eyes over my naked body.

"You left your heels on."

I smiled. "I did."

He grinned back at me, smoldering and confident. "You're so fucking sexy, Rachel. I can't believe I wasted my whole senior year *not* dating you."

I put my hands on either side of his chest and pushed myself up onto the bed. His cock was mere inches away from me. I look down to see how close it actually was, and my pussy was wet and glistening with my juices. I was so close to fucking the boy of my dreams, the boy I'd had a crush on since the middle of my junior year.

I leaned forward, my pelvis arcing up slightly, then I lowered myself down—and *bingo*. His hard cock slipped inside of me.

Oh shit. This would be my first time. It didn't *feel* to me like my first time—I'd definitely used the O-Quest on myself frequently enough for it to almost feel like I'd already lost my V-card. But suddenly all the stuff my friends told me—*it always hurts the first time, he won't know what he's doing, he came in about ten seconds, just get through it*—went racing through my brain.

Just shut up, girls. You never got to fuck your dream boy.

It wasn't the sharp, stabbing pain a couple of my friends had told me about, but it was a stretching, tight feeling. I closed my eyes and breathed out, but my exhalation came low and slow and guttural. *Fuck*.

"Oh, oh, oh God, my beautiful girl," Jalen said, his arms wrapping around me. "I've been waiting for this moment for so long."

"Put two fingers on top of my clit, Jalen," I whispered to him. He opened his eyes and smiled at me. He seemed a little surprised that I was asking him to do something. Maybe all the girls he'd been with had been silent. He moved his right hand just above my clit and slowly ran two fingers back and forth, barely touching it.

"Harder," I said. "I like it harder than that."

He applied a little more pressure.

"More," I moaned, "that feels good, Jalen." It felt good enough that the tight feeling inside my sex was turning into more pleasure than pain. It was similar to what the O-Quest did, but the angle of his cock inside me was a lot different than the shaft of the vibrator.

"Oh my God, Jalen, your fingers are fucking *amazing*."

With his left hand, he lifted my chin up again, and kissed me on the lips, slow and gentle and sensual. I raised myself up, but not so high that he'd slip out, and lowered my body onto his rigid shaft again. I took my time sliding down and closed my eyes. His fingers were back, playing with my clit just the way I'd told him to.

I'd never had any type of connection like this with any of

the guys I'd dated before. Well, I mean, I'd never gone this far with them, but even making out with them, or when I'd give them a hand job or blow job, or when they fingered me, I never felt this kind of connection. Even though I suppose I'd have to technically call myself a virgin, I'd seen a fair amount of penises. Jalen wasn't markedly bigger than any of the others, not noticeably thicker, not noticeably different aside from skin color. But there was definitely something different and something better. He was moving his hips, just slightly, and the very slight curvature of his cock was hitting me in *just* the right place inside, a place my O-Quest had never come close to, and a place that even with my fingers I had to contort myself in all kinds of ways to get the right kind of friction.

"That—that—oh my God—that's the *perfect* spot," I said, my breath coming in shorter and shorter gasps.

"You feel so good," Jalen said, so low that I almost didn't hear him.

We got into a rhythm, and the band downstairs started a faster song that matched our tempo. It's like the band was magically attuned to our sex, like everything worked together to make sure that *this* time, Jalen and I found each other in everything: in the night, in the stars, in the music, in the tempo, and that everything in the universe would work together for the two of us to share the ultimate sexual experience that had been building between us.

With the rhythm shaking the walls on the downbeat every time I came crashing down against Jalen's pelvis, I felt something start to build inside me. Jalen had added his left thumb, making slow half-circles just under my clit, adding to the first two fingers of his right hand still putting the sustained pressure just above, and the almost-but-not-quite-direct pressure was pushing the limits of how much pleasure I could feel before having an orgasm. I'd had excellent orgasms with my vibrator, and even a few orgasms when the guys I dated touched me with their fingers or tongues in the right places. But this was different. The weird stretching feeling was still there, but something very similar to my other orgasms, but not exactly the same, was coming up underneath it.

It started slow, and I kept grinding on Jalen, vaguely aware that every time I ground my hips, his fingers were getting the edge of my clit, and it was driving me crazy that it wasn't getting me off immediately, and yet the feeling was building in intensity so much, more and more and more, with each time I circled.

Jalen's breath was coming faster and faster. His eyes floated closed, and I let mine close too. I leaned forward a little more, so there wasn't any more room for his left hand with his thumb. Jalen put his left hand on my breast, playing delicately with my nipple, sending little jolts of electricity through my torso that alternated with the pleasure circles between my legs. His thumb might not have been there, but I was getting skin-to-skin contact, and his fingers went down just a millimeter or two, and the pleasure cranked up even more.

"Oh," I whispered. "Oh, Jalen, right there, I'm about to come."

"I *want* you to come, my beautiful girl," he said.

"I'm—uhh—" Then I took a breath and squealed. Not loud, but it was definitely a squeal, and the sensations burst from me. My circles with my hips got faster, and Jalen's cock inside me kept getting me in the right place, and it felt like my orgasm went on *forever*. I wanted to lose myself in that feeling, where I was just falling, falling, falling into Jalen's beautiful body, into his kisses, and the cinnamon and grapefruit scent when I nuzzled into his neck, and into everything he could do to me.

I couldn't tell when it ended, but I opened my eyes and found myself lying on Jalen's chest. My hips had stopped circling, though I could still feel him inside me.

"Holy shit, Jalen," I said, out of breath. "I was worried that I'd gotten you on such a pedestal in my head that there's no way it could have met my expectations. But I can't believe it. That wasn't just better than I expected, it's forcing me to recalibrate my whole goddamn sex evaluation system." I pushed myself up and looked in his eyes. "Did you—?"

His eyes were sparkling. "Hell yeah, I came," he said. "Right when you started to orgasm. It put me over the edge. Fuck—you were hot when I saw you on the porch tonight. You were *super* hot when I saw you naked. But the sight of you coming while riding on my dick? That's the hottest thing I've *ever* seen. I couldn't last for another half a second after that."

"So," I said, "will we be okay on a date now? Can we talk about things without getting all tongue-tied?"

He laughed. "Damn, I hope so. If we get all anxious and weird, we can always downshift into making out."

"*Just* making out?"

"Uh—no, not *just* making out. I didn't want to presume anything."

"Really? After that fantastic frenzy of fucking? I'm down for more than making out. Whenever you get a little nervous, I'll do that instead of a shoulder massage any day of the week."

Jalen smacked my ass lightly and said, "All right, let's get to the next stage of the evening and raise up for a minute so that I can go clean up."

"Oh, right. Sure." I raise my hips a little and he slid out of me. The sensation was a little odd, definitely different than when I removed the vibrator.

"Thanks. I'll be right back." Jalen rolled out from under me and went into the connected bathroom.

I rolled on my back and stared at the ceiling. I'd just had sex with my fantasy boy. I didn't even remember the name of the person whose room I was in. Did Jalen's brother's friend expect Jalen to have sex in his bed? Given Jalen's status as the Eighth Wonder of the World, he probably did.

Jalen and I broke down that barrier between us. Maybe Elaine and Eric were right—maybe we *did* have to have sex before we could be real around each other. What would we do next? It was too late on a Thursday night to have a real date. Potentially, we could go downstairs and make an appearance at the party. Maybe I could even find Gina.

Maybe Jalen would like me to stay in his borrowed-for-a-semester room with him. I didn't know if Jalen had any Friday classes or basketball practice. I didn't even know if he had a game this weekend. I didn't know if Jalen expected me to stay over, or if he wanted me to go.

But I was no longer nervous, or anxious, or wondering if I'd ruin my chances with him. I mean, he said he wanted a date with me, but even if he'd just wanted to get me into bed, it wasn't like I would see him around campus and feel like crawling into a hole. It wasn't like he'd spread rumors about me. And I got him into bed, too, which I really wanted. He was just as much of a dirty ho as I was.

Jalen opened the door of the bathroom and came to the bed. I swung my legs out of bed and stood up.

"Hey," Jalen said, "you're not leaving, are you?"

I raised my eyebrows. "Not naked, I'm not."

"You could stay. At least for a little while longer."

I smiled, and a sense of relief surprisingly washed over me. "I'll be right back."

I went into Jalen's bathroom. When I'd finished, as I washed my hands in the sink, I looked up.

Huh. The girl in the mirror staring back at me looked... happier. I tilted my head and kept noticing new things about her. Her skin glowed in a way I really hadn't seen before. She looked relaxed. Her forehead didn't have the usual creases in it. There wasn't a line between her eyebrows where she would constantly furrow her brow. I rinsed my hands and turned the water off, then stood up.

I was still the same curvy girl Jalen knew in high school. I hadn't magically lost the thirty pounds I'd been wanting to lose. The diet I'd started when I arrived at college hadn't taken four inches off my waist.

I turned to the side and looked at my profile in the mirror. What was it that Jalen saw in me? Was it just my big boobs and my big ass? They weren't particularly awesome, except for being on the larger side. I tilted my head the other way. I didn't *hate* my boobs. For me, that might be the most body-positive thing I'd thought about myself since my date with Jalen a year ago. I saw the curves of my body in the mirror. And of course my calves. I *did* like my calves.

No one could accuse me of being built like a boy. I was

curvier than the other women he'd dated before, but maybe Jalen appreciated how feminine I looked. Maybe he even preferred it.

I spun and looked at myself from the other side, but it wasn't that different. I put my hands on my stomach and sucked in my belly. I didn't look half bad, actually. I was getting goose flesh from the chill in the air, and the fact that I wasn't wearing anything. I dropped my hands and checked my face for signs of wrinkles or smeared makeup, and again I was surprised by how contented I looked.

I opened the door and walked out into the bedroom naked.

Jalen lay on the bed, sitting up and leaning against the headboard. The sheet was pulled around his waist, but it was off his hip slightly, and I could tell he was naked underneath. His face lit up when he saw me.

"Hey, Rachel," he said, "want to come back to bed?"

I could hear the band downstairs start another song, this one a reggae tune, slow and mellow. "Yeah," I said, and I got in next to him.

He pushed himself down so that he was lying on his back, and I wrapped myself around him, my hand on his chest, and my leg draped over him. His cock, now at less than half-mast, rested against my thigh, my head on his shoulder. His skin was surprisingly soft, and his body was warm. It felt like home, like a natural place to be, even though I was in a strange room in a strange house in a strange city with a boy I didn't even know that well.

"You good?" he asked.

"Yeah," I said. "I like this."

He pulled me closer. "Me too."

The water pulses and I startle. I've been daydreaming in the shower for a while. As I finish rinsing off, I sigh. It's nice to remember my first time with Jalen.

When I get out of the shower, the clock on the bedside table says 9:28 PM. Crap, I spent much longer in the shower than I'd intended. I'll have to hurry with my hair and makeup if I want to be ready before Jalen gets home.

I wrap myself in a towel and dry my hair, brushing it out. I considered doing something special with it, maybe an updo, something that would show off my neck and shoulders, but Jalen likes my hair down. It was down the day in high school when he first asked me out, and it was down the night Gina and I showed up to the house party at Arrowhead U, the first night Jalen and I spent together. I have to use a little more product for my hair to look vivacious and flirty rather than the usual work look.

I rub body lotion on, too, and it smells faintly of coconut oil, reminding me of a late summer weekend at Lake Arrowhead. I check my phone; it's 9:47, and I have no messages from Jalen, which means he won't be too late. I don't expect him home at ten on the dot, but I shouldn't have to wait much longer.

I take out the two pieces of lingerie from the drawer. I'm not really into either of them. The see-through babydoll is a little *too* forward. But the black silk chemise is just about perfect, now that I know I won't be spending more than fifteen minutes or so waiting for Jalen. It's short and sexy and sleeveless, and I love the way it feels against my skin.

Hmm. Maybe I can do heels tonight too. I close my eyes

and picture Jalen in that sexy gray suit. The cut of the trousers on it are especially nice. I'm not sure how long he'll be *in* those trousers after he sees me. I look around the shoe rack until I see them, the heels I wore to the party at Arrowhead U fifteen years before.

They're not the most fashionable shoes anymore—the style is definitely from last decade. But I bet Jalen won't care. When he sees me in these stilettos, he'll remember back to that room, and that night, and then I hope he'll take me in his arms, and the three months of frustration will start to recede.

I touch up my lipstick. It's been a while since I spent this much time getting ready before seeing Jalen. I know it doesn't *really* matter to him, but it makes me feel a little more confident. Plus, Jalen will see the effort and he'll know how much I want to be with him tonight, to feel his body next to mine, to make love for the first time in a few months.

I look at myself in the mirror, and it definitely looks like I'm trying to seduce my husband. I take a deep breath and open the door.

There's a light coming out of the office. That's weird. Didn't I turn that off when I walked out of the room?

I hadn't closed the document with the Werewolf In Phoenix story, either. I guess I should probably do that too. I'll probably be distracting Jalen enough so that he won't even look twice at my computer, but I'd rather not take the chance of him seeing it.

I walk into the office and stop in my tracks.

Jalen is sitting at the computer.

Reading my story.

HOMECOMING

"Oh shit," I say.

Jalen doesn't turn around. "Hey, babe," he says faintly. I see the screen in front of him. He's at the part where Dr. Rachel Bennet is trying not to touch Jeff's massive, comatose erection.

There's no other way for him to interpret what he's reading. I'm the curvaceous doctor, and he's the huge-dicked, erect patient.

I want to crawl in a hole and die.

"What...," he begins.

Then he scrolls down, reading more, the silence stretching between us.

Oh my God, the part with Nurse Alicia being sent out of the room—this part is after that scene. He'll know I put his ex-girlfriend—no, now his *boss*—in this smutty story.

"Did you—" he starts to say, but his voice breaks. He clears his throat. "Did you write this?"

"Yes," I say, my voice small. "But, I, uh—I can explain."

He doesn't tear his eyes away from the screen. "Wow."

I can't tell if his expression is a positive reaction, or if it's judgmental and negative. Besides, I have *no idea* how to explain it to him. How will I spin this so my story doesn't sound like the ramblings of a needy, desperate woman?

I feel the tips of my ears burn with shame as he keeps reading, and finally I take a step forward. "You—you don't have to read that, you know."

"Why not?" he whispers. As I walk toward him, I see his eyes are wide, almost like he's drinking this in. Wait—is he *enjoying* this?

"Were you embarrassed to show this to m—" He turns his head to look at me, and his eyes get even wider when he sees that I'm wearing nothing but lingerie and the same stilettos I wore the first night we were together. "Wait— what's going on?"

I suddenly feel exposed—in more than just my choice of outfit. "I've—uh—I've missed you, Jalen."

His face softens. "I've missed you too."

"You've been in Europe for too long."

"You're right."

I rake my eyes over his body. Even seated, he looks good. He's still in his suit, and he looks debonair and powerful. I clear my throat. "There are a lot of things I'd like to change about your travel schedule, but for right now, I just want to be with you. Feel your body next to mine."

He tilts his head as if he's pointing to the screen with his chin. "When did you write this?"

I pause. "Well, I started the first story during your first trip to Zurich. We hadn't ever gone that long without, you know, being intimate. And I couldn't really stand it."

"*First* story?"

"Oh." I look down at the floor and see my heels, sexy, yes, but they made it hard to balance on the carpet in the office. "I mean, they're not complete novels or anything. I actually haven't even finished one all the way through. I've got four stories so far."

He runs his hands over his hair, cropped close to his scalp. "Four stories. Just since I've started traveling to Switzerland?"

"Like I said, none of them are finished. Listen, Jalen, I know I didn't tell you about them, but I just missed you so much I had to write these stories about you and me."

He smiles. "Yeah, I was pretty sure I was Jeff in this one."

"I kind of had a whole *Pride and Prejudice* thing happening."

He nods. "That's what I figured. Bennet and Darcy."

"I know these stories are silly—"

"Silly?" Jalen stands up. For a highly regarded college basketball player, he's not that tall—only about half a foot taller than I am in these stilettos—but the way he carries himself, it's like he's towering over me.

And then I look down.

Oh, he's got an erection. It's tenting out the front of his trousers obscenely.

"Your werewolf story *isn't* silly."

"It's not?"

"No, it isn't. That dream that Dr. Bennet has with the sex swing? That's hot as hell."

The relief washes over me. "Hot as hell?"

He takes a step toward me. "That's what I said. And *you're* hot as hell too."

I smile, but I feel it falter on my face.

"Hey, hey, Rachel, what's the matter?"

I swallow hard. "Nothing."

He looks at me. "Yes, there is."

I hesitate and then barrel ahead. "I'm so—I'm so lonely with you traveling so much. But it's not just that. It's like I feel like we're not connecting anymore, even when you're home. And—and then that bitch Alicia shows up, and she's your new boss, and I just feel so *powerless* about everything."

Jalen wraps his arms around me. "I'm so sorry," he whispers in my ear.

"I know you're out there working your ass off so we can have money for the IVF and for a bigger house," I say, "but none of it will mean anything if we can't be together."

"I want to be with you," he says, "forever. I hate being in Europe without you. I'm going crazy too. I've never been as lonely as I am when I go back to the hotel in Zurich on Friday night, with the weekend stretching out before me, with nothing to look forward to but two Skype calls with you. Yes, those video chats are my favorite parts of the day, but it doesn't compare at all to being with you at home."

He's caressing my back, and as many crazy emotions as are going through my head, my body is responding to him. I'm moving my hips in a slow circle, and I reach down and unbuckle his belt and undo the clasp above his fly. "I missed being with you, and being held, and I missed you kissing me," I say, "and I really need you inside me right now."

He steps back, belt undone, removing his jacket, and then hooking it on the rack next to the bookcase. He takes my hand, and then he sits down in the chair.

"What are you doing?"

"If you hadn't noticed, your story was getting me very

aroused," he said. "Maybe we should sit together and read it." He smirks. "Doctor Rachel."

"And just where will I sit, patient Darcy?"

He reaches under the bottom hem of my chemise and pulls my lacy panties down around my thighs. Then he pushes his pants down to his knees. When he leans back in the chair, his penis salutes me, rapt at attention. "My lap is available."

"I see." I'm still standing, and I lean over and kiss him, shaking my hips and legs so my panties fall to my ankles. I break from the kiss and carefully step out of my panties, making sure not to catch the ridiculous heel points on the lace.

"You're the sexiest woman I've ever seen," Jalen growls as he watches me.

When I've kicked the panties to the side, I step in front of him. "You're the sexiest man I've ever seen."

"It's a good thing we found each other."

I turn around, facing the screen, my knees surrounding his. My butt stares him in the face.

"That ass, though," he says, groaning with pleasure.

"You like it, huh?"

In response, he puts his hands on my hips and pulls me toward him gently. I carefully sit down, my ass on his thighs, the tip of his rigid cock grazing the small of my back.

"I've missed this." I shift my weight, left and right, and I feel the tip of his cock move softly, slowly, subtly, over my lower back. Jalen's breaths come a little faster.

"Do you want me to read to you, Jalen?"

"That would be lovely," he says, low and guttural.

"Where did you leave off?"

"Right where Dr. Bennet realizes that he's only erect when she's in the room. Right after she told off that bitchy nurse."

"Are you ready, baby?"

"I've never been more ready, Rachel."

AN AMERICAN WEREWOLF IN
PHOENIX, PART II

*F*or the next two weeks, Dr. Bennet couldn't figure out what to do with Jeff. Every time she walked in the room to check on him, he was as erect as a lightning rod and she was drawn to it like a bolt of electricity. It took all of her self-control to stop from stripping out of her white coat and blue scrubs and climbing on top of him. She asked the other nurses if they'd noticed anything unusual. They'd all noticed a change in his musculature, but every one of them dismissed it as impossible. As for Nurse Alicia, she had called in sick the last two times she was scheduled to work the same shift as Dr. Bennet.

The well-regarded neurosurgeon was usually able to avoid the temptation of Jeff's huge, beautiful cock by asking a nurse to attend to him; however, on two occasions the nurses were busy with other patients. The doctor had to go check on Jeff herself. The first time, she noticed that Jeff now had a full, thick beard, not week-old craggily growth, but facial hair that might take the average man a month or two to properly grow. She noted this on her tablet and then uncovered the blanket from Jeff's body. Again, Dr. Bennet noticed his erection tenting his gown, and she had to fight the temptation to remove it to see the large member. She'd even gone so far as to grab the lower hem before she stopped herself.

Three days later, Dr. Bennet walked into his hospital room, reviewing the still-unusual blood work results on her tablet.

"Where am I?"

Dr. Bennet's head snapped up and she nearly dropped the tablet in surprise.

"You're awake," she said simply, trying to keep the surprise out of her voice.

"I'm awake?" he said, staring in confusion at the IV tubes coming from his arm. "What does that mean?"

"You're in Phoenix General Hospital," replied the doctor. Jeff had kind eyes, but the unmasked confusion there was difficult for her to see without the pain of sympathy swimming over her. "I'm Dr. Rachel Bennet. I'm the neurosurgeon assigned to your case."

"Neurosurgeon? What am I doing here?"

"You were attacked." The neurologist explained everything that was in the report: the wolf attack, the rescuers in the pickup truck. She burned with curiosity about whether or not his gorgeous cock was still hard now that he was awake.

"I need to use the bathroom," Jeff said.

"Can you move?" Dr. Bennet asked. "You've been in bed for two weeks, and often people in your condition—"

Jeff pushed himself up to a sitting position and swung his legs out from under the blankets. Sure enough, his huge cock tented the front of the hospital gown again. He didn't exhibit any of the weakness or muscle usage issues that Dr. Bennet had expected.

"I should probably call a nurse in to assist you," she said, trying like crazy not to stare at his crotch, but not succeeding.

Jeff glanced up at her as she averted her eyes, and then he looked down into his lap. "Oh damn," he blurted. "I'm so sorry, doctor. It just kind of happened. Like, you know, the morning erection guys get. I guess I've been in a coma for so long it sort of combined all the morning erections I'd missed into one."

Doctor Rachel's eyes were still on Jeff's erection. "That—that doesn't usually happen," she said, her voice distant. "But, please, don't worry about it. It's a simple reactive condition in many patients who, uh, wake up. Nothing I haven't seen before." *Since I've seen it before, for sure, in all its glory.*

Dr. Bennet went to the intercom and called a nurse in, thanking her lucky stars that Nurse Alicia had called in sick again. A nurse named Sonia entered, shocked that Jeff had woken up without the machines alerting her to the change in status, but she quickly put a smile on her face and went to work assisting Jeff with his IV tubes, hooking them over the handles of the wheeled cart. Unlike Dr. Bennet, the nurse kept her eyes up and didn't blink at his unusual hardened state.

"I'll be fine," Jeff said, when the nurse entered the bathroom with him.

"Possibly," the nurse replied, "but that's usually not the case when someone wakes from a coma. If you fall and hurt yourself and I'm not in there, my afternoon will be spent in paperwork hell, and then I'll be mad at you." She laughed, her eyes twinkling merrily, and Jeff managed a wan smile.

When the bathroom door was closed, Dr. Bennet let out the deep breath she'd been holding. Things might change when Jeff woke, but if anything, the incredibly delicious erection attached to an actual moving, live, sentient body was even more of a turn-on.

Nurse Sonia obviously wasn't affected by Jeff's condition. Dr. Bennet wondered if the cause for that impressive hard-on was some sort of pheromone, or some kind of amino acid deficiency. Her mind raced, trying to land on some plausible scientific explanation, but couldn't. It was like she had seen his massive cock and *imprinted* on it, like a baby duck seeing its mother for the first time.

She was stuck rooted to the spot. Part of her wanted to get as far away as humanly possible, to not only save her career, but to save herself from getting bonded to Jeff himself. If he asked her to be his slave, chained to the bed face down and rutting multiple times a day, she feared she'd not only say yes, but she'd buy the chains herself.

No. I've got to get out of here. I can't be around him.

She just had to get through one more day. He was strong enough to go to the bathroom by himself. He'd be out of the ICU as soon as a bed opened up, which might be as early as the afternoon. She'd never have to see him again in a professional setting.

Now, if she just happened to meet him by chance in a neighborhood bar, that was another matter entirely. She wouldn't have to stop herself from doing anything. She could buy him a drink, then another, then drive him home and have her way with him. Or perhaps she'd run into him in the produce department at the grocery store where he usually shopped, and she would squeeze the cantaloupes suggestively, or run her hand over a cucumber seductively, licking her lips, maybe even have him cook her dinner before fucking him on the sofa. She could ride him as he held her, his strong arms wrapped around her back, and she'd come, stronger than she had in the shower by herself.

There was a flush from the bathroom, and a moment later the door opened. Jeff led the way, cheeks a bit red, wheeling his IV cart behind him. Dr. Bennet stole a glance at his crotch. He seemed to have lost his erection, and she felt both relief and disappointment.

"No problems at all with balance," Nurse Sonia said. "I've never seen anything like it before, where a patient wakes up from a coma and it's like he was never even unconscious. He's not even exhibiting any signs of brain trauma." She didn't mention his erection as he went into the bathroom, of course, but Jeff wouldn't meet her eyes.

Dr. Bennet nodded. "That—" She choked on the first word that came out of her mouth. Her throat was dry, and her pussy was screaming for attention. "That's unusual, but it's wonderful news. We can arrange for you to be moved to a regular room, just for observation. At least two more nights. Patients who come out of comas often have symptoms that make themselves known several hours later." She was stretching the truth a bit, but she wanted him out of her ICU and out of the hospital—and in her bed, his face between her legs.

Jeff turned to the sink in the room and began to wash his

hands. He saw his reflection in the mirror, and touched his full beard, wonderment in his eyes.

"Doctor," he said, "how long was I out?"

Dr. Bennet cleared her throat. "About two weeks."

"Two weeks?" His jaw hung open in shock. "I can't grow a beard like this in just two weeks."

Dr. Rachel Bennet shrugged. "I don't have an explanation either."

The nurse nodded and looked at Dr. Bennet. "There's another patient I need to attend to. Do you mind if I step out for a moment?"

"Thank you," Dr. Bennet said. "That will be all for now. I appreciate the assistance."

Jeff continued to stare at his reflection in the mirror above the sink. His eyes were full of a million questions, as if he barely recognized himself.

"How are you feeling?" Dr. Bennet ventured. "I know this must all seem a bit surreal."

Jeff nodded, still locked on his reflection. "Yeah, doctor, this is surreal for sure. Honestly, though, I'm feeling better than I've ever have in my life." His stomach rumbled. "Well, I'm hungry, for one thing. And I could definitely use a glass of water." He put his right hand on his left shoulder and rotated it. "You know, I broke this shoulder falling off my bike when I was fifteen years old. It broke in three places and it took them two surgeries to reconstruct it, and it really hasn't been right since. Sort of a dull ache. I don't even notice the pain most of the time." He raised his arm up, taking care not to put strain on the intravenous tubes, and gingerly shook it and then made a wide, slow circle.

"What are you doing?" Dr. Bennet asked.

"I haven't been able to make a complete circle with my arm since the accident," Jeff said, almost to himself. "And now I don't have any pain at all. None."

Dr. Bennet narrowed her eyes. This was most unusual.

"I'll tell you something else, Doctor," Jeff said, turning around to face her, looking right in her eyes. "Doctor Bennet, right?" he ventured.

Oh God. She melted in his gaze. "Please, call me Rachel," she said. Then she hesitated. *Call me Rachel?* She'd never asked a patient to call her by her first name before. She shook her head.

"Well, I twisted my knee pretty badly last month," Jeff said. "I couldn't put weight on it for a couple of days, and I was worried—" He started to walk forward and then stopped suddenly, and looked down at the crotch of his hospital gown tenting out again.

Dr. Bennet followed his eyes. "Oh," she said softly, parting her lips delicately. She tried to shake off her lusty thoughts and caught a glimpse of herself in the mirror. She barely recognized herself, because the woman staring back her was pretty. More than pretty. Even in the ugly royal blue scrubs under the white coat, she could see her lush curves. Although she wore minimal makeup for her job, and today was no exception, her face was heart-shaped, with full lips and high cheekbones. She wasn't skinny enough to walk the runway, but she was attractive. Suddenly she realized how Nurse Alicia could be so cruel to her, and how a patient that she barely knew could be standing three feet in front of her, his cock at full attention.

"I'm—I'm sorry," Jeff gasped. "I've never had anything like this happen before."

Dr. Bennet couldn't take her eyes off his rigid dick, and she took a step forward, feeling that sashay in her wide, full hips. "Don't worry about it," she said, trying as hard as she could to look Jeff in the eyes. "It's an involuntary reaction."

She heard a guttural, sexual growl in Jeff's throat. That got her attention off his cock, and she found herself staring into his eyes.

"It doesn't *feel* like an involuntary reaction," Jeff said in a low, gravelly voice. "It feels like I'll throw you down on this bed and fuck you the way you've wanted me to ever since you first saw me."

Dr. Bennet made a startled gurgling noise in her throat. "How—how did you know?" she asked in a whisper.

He sniffed the air, subtly. It wasn't menacing or creepy. Dr. Bennet couldn't quite make out the terms, but it felt like simple information gathering. "I don't know how I can tell," he said quietly. "But I can somehow sense it. I can somehow sense what you need, what you want." He was quiet for another moment. "You *do* want me, Doctor. You want me to take control over you. You want me to tell you what to do to please me."

Dr. Bennet closed her eyes. This couldn't be happening. Why couldn't this happen on an online-meeting date instead of a work situation? Why did the first man she was this incredibly drawn to have to be a *patient*?

"I can't," she whispered. "You're a patient. I'll get in so much trouble."

Jeff shuddered a bit, as if he were holding himself back. "Of course," he said. "Of course you can't do anything about it right now. I—I don't even know what's come over me. There's something in the air. It draws me to you, makes me want to do things to you." He took a step toward her. "Dirty things. Naughty things."

"Please fuck me," Rachel whispered.

❧

"I'm ready, baby," Jalen whispers in my ear. I reach behind me, and I wrap my hand around his shaft. He's ready, all right, and I've already felt the telltale drops of precum on the small of my back.

I lift myself up, still holding onto his shaft, and push my ass back toward Jalen. I set my weight down into his lap, and aim his cock right into my dripping wet pussy. I expect a little more resistance, but after two months without him inside me, and two and a half weeks since I'd seen him in person, I'm even more ready than he is. He sucks in a breath as he enters me.

"Ooh, Jalen, does that feel good?"

"Fuck, Rachel, you're so goddamn gorgeous."

"You feel so good inside me, baby."

"*Don't* stop reading."

"Are you sure you can—unnhh—handle both the book and me at the same time?"

"I've never been more turned on in my life, Rachel. Keep going."

❧

"Please fuck me," Dr. Rachel Bennet said.

Jeff D'Arcy took one more step forward—

The nurse who had helped Jeff to the bathroom came

back in. "Thank you for staying in here while I handled the situation back there, doctor. I can take over—"

Doctor Rachel Bennet held up a hand, commanding silence. "No need to thank me, Sonia. I've uncovered a potential issue here, and I'll need to make sure we don't have complications."

"Certainly, doctor. Do you need assistance?"

Dr. Bennet shook her head. "Not at the moment, Sonia. You can tend to the rest of your patients. I'll let you know if —when—I need assistance."

Jeff looked at Sonia, and then Dr. Bennet closed her eyes.

And with a sudden terrific decrescendo, everything went dark and silent.

No medical machines whirring.

No sound of breathing.

No distant phones ringing.

Just dark and quiet.

Then softly a *thump, thump, thump*, repeated over and over, like a heartbeat.

It was *her* heartbeat, beating in time with his.

Like she'd been dropped into a sensory deprivation tank.

She floated there. Could she open her eyes? Did she even *want* to open her eyes? She was surrounded by just nothingness, a void. She tried to speak, but nothing came out.

I'm sorry, said Jeff's voice inside her head.

Oh, that's strange, she thought. Then, thinking at the voice, *Where am I?*

I'm not quite sure how I did it, Jeff said. *I didn't want to cause you any harm.*

I don't understand. Had she really connected with him

cosmically? Was it the baby-duck-imprinting thing she had felt before?

You didn't imprint on me, Doctor Bennet. I imprinted on you. Your scent, your DNA, your everything—it's matched perfectly with me, with this new thing I'm becoming.

Wait—what? Imprinted on me? What new thing you're becoming?

I don't understand it all, either, Doctor Bennet.

Please, call me Rachel. If you've imprinted on me, at least you can call me by my first name.

Sure, that makes sense. Rachel it is, then.

Where am I? How did I get here?

I've had to separate your consciousness from you for a while. It was getting dangerous. You were about to do something you'd regret.

Dr. Bennet remembered. She'd just sent Sonia out of the room. When the nurse first came back in, Dr. Bennet was relieved that there was someone else there to take the pressure off her and make her pull away from the magnetic attraction with Jeff's huge erection. But the curvy neurosurgeon didn't grab onto that lifeline. She'd taken it and tossed it overboard, along with any chance she'd had of keeping her job. She might even go to jail, depending on how much coercion a jury could be convinced of. *Thank you for rescuing me.*

It is not me who rescued you, Rachel. If I hadn't imprinted on someone before my transformation was complete, I would have died. I mean, the wolf that attacked me meant to kill me, but as he was interrupted before he could do it, I began a transformation instead.

If Rachel had been in her a corporeal body, she would have shaken her head. *So you have to be mated before you can even live? And—transformed into what?*

I only understand parts of it. But it seems that I'll be transformed into a beast. Part man, part wolf.

A werewolf.

They don't call themselves werewolves, and there are some essential differences to the mythology, but yes, that's basically it. It's the easiest thing to make you understand what's happening with me, anyway.

Where am I?

I—I am not entirely sure. You're somewhere safe. Somewhere you won't get fired, if that's what you're worried about.

What happened? Did you stop time or something?

I brought you here, Jeff said simply.

And now what happens?

Only things that you want to happen, Rachel.

Only things I want to happen? I want you to fuck me. I want your huge cock inside me, pulsating, throbbing. I want you to kiss my neck right above my collarbone while you're sliding your huge dick in and out of me, driving me wild with pleasure. I want my hands running through your hair as you wrap your arm around me and put your hand on the back of my head.

And then the world all around Dr. Bennet got lighter. It was all gray, like thick fog, so dense nothing could be seen. She started to be able to feel her body. Touch was available, but no sight, no sound. Dr. Bennet wiggled her fingers and toes. She lifted her left arm and then her right, and then she bent her knees. Her feet still didn't feel any resistance, and Dr. Bennet still floated along in the gray nothingness.

Then.

A hand grasped hers, gently, softly, like a lover might. *Jeff?*

Yes, it's me, Rachel.

I don't know what's going on.

Are you afraid?

She almost replied that she was, except she had an overwhelming sensation of calmness. A calm that had been there since she had found herself in the darkness.

No, she said. *I expected to be, but I'm not.*

That's good, he said. *That means you're the one.*

I'm the what?

Then Dr. Rachel Bennet felt his lips press against hers, soft but firm, and with an urgency behind the kiss that she'd never felt before.

She opened her mouth to let his tongue explore hers, and he obliged, and Dr. Bennet moaned, although she could only hear it in her mind.

That's good, he said, not breaking the kiss. *Let yourself go. Let your desire flow into the space between us.*

Let it go? How would I even—

Then Dr. Bennet felt her body release, and his body, hard with muscle, soft with emotion, sinewy and delicate at the same time, pressed against her soft, lush curves. First his hands on her back roamed from her shoulder blades down to her ass. Then she felt his chest press against her too, her nipples hard against his pecs, and then their stomachs were flush together, his hard abdominal muscles and her beautiful soft belly, touching the six-pack two by two.

She felt the tip of his penis, insistent, touch her about a quarter of an inch below her belly button. It felt warmer than the rest of him, and its heat spread throughout her belly and her sex. Dr. Rachel Bennet began bucking her hips, trying to reach down to slip his cock inside her.

Not yet, my dear, he said, still not breaking from the kiss. *It's not time just yet.*

I want it so bad, Dr. Bennet said. *I want your big cock inside my pussy like your tongue is inside my mouth. Explore every part of me, Jeff. Make me come over and over, like I was doing in the shower every day after I saw your huge cock in the ICU.*

She felt his thighs rub against hers, and then his legs, and then her toes were touching his ankles, and he was touching Rachel from top to bottom. The sensations drove her crazy.

I can't figure out what this is. She put her tongue in his mouth too, and he let her.

I can't either. I'm just going with it.

Does this mean—does this mean we're together for good? Does it mean you'll turn me into a werewolf too? Or that we'll both die at the next full moon?

I don't know, Jeff said. *I don't know if imprinting on a human is okay, or if you have to transform too.*

I'm not sure I care, Jeff—not as long as you're inside me.

And he growled, low in his throat, and then with a gasp and a thrust, he was inside her.

Dr. Bennet threw her head back in the sudden pleasure. She'd had orgasms before, but this was unreal, and the rush wasn't even at its pinnacle yet. The release of energy and magic when he entered her created a wash of tingling over her whole body. She let herself go completely and she felt herself tumbling, although she had no idea which way was up. She felt him both everywhere on her body and nowhere, except for the continuous luscious sensation of him sliding in and out of her pussy. Dr. Bennet became vaguely aware that he was playing with her clit with his fingers, and the physical pleasure kept ramping up.

She felt his lips on the side of her neck, on the side of her face behind her cheek, on her ear, and then his hot breath. "I know we just met, Rachel, but I'll be with you forever. Love is different on this plane, my beautiful one, and this is it. You haven't felt this before because you haven't been *able* to feel it before."

꧁

Jalen had moved his right hand between my legs, and he started lightly rubbing my clit with his first two fingers. I had trouble focusing on the words. "...because you haven't been *able* to—Unnh, oh God, Jalen. *Right fucking there.* More pressure, baby. Just a little more."

"Keep reading, honey," he whispered.

"Oh my God, I can't, Jalen, I'm about to come."

꧁

"I'm not sure," Dr. Bennet gasped, "if I can stand much more of this." The electricity was coursing through her body from her sex and radiated outward. She could feel the buzz of her arousal with his hot breath in her ear, alternating with the electricity coming from her pussy. "I can't stand it anymore," she moaned.

Dr. Rachel Bennet orgasmed, and he did too, filling her pussy with his seed, with his sweetness, and she could feel her muscles clench and let go, clench and let go, as his cock pulsed, once, twice, three times. She lost count of how many times he released inside of her.

It's like I've been with him forever.

Like everything up to this point was simply waiting for Jeff, waiting for him to meet her. Nothing in her life had prepared her for this, and nothing else, in this gray world, mattered except for the two of them.

"I can hear you talk now," she whispered into his ear, when their orgasms had subsided. "You're not speaking directly into my brain anymore."

"Things will start to clarify," Jeff said.

Slowly the gray cloud obscuring her vision began to dissipate, and she could feel herself lying down on her back, Jeff on top. The mist lightened, and Dr. Rachel Bennet and Mr. Jeff Darcy were in her bedroom. They were both naked on her bed. The room was illuminated only by the thin rays of twilight filtering through the blinds on the window above the headboard.

"Here we are," Jeff said.

"What happened to the day?" Dr. Bennet asked. "It wasn't even ten in the morning."

"I was transferred around eleven, and they released me this afternoon," Jeff said. "Sonia never left the ICU room. You did the rest of your rounds. And then as we were both leaving for the day, we ran into each other in the parking lot. I was walking to the bus stop, and you were getting in your car. You offered to give me a ride home."

Rachel shook her head. "But I couldn't resist you."

Jeff smiled. "And I couldn't resist you, either. So we kissed in the car, and we drove to your apartment, and my clothes were halfway off before we even got in the door."

"And then we fell into bed together and made love," Dr. Rachel Bennet said. "And we'll make love for hours."

"Yes," Jeff said, "we'll make love for hours."

ANGER MANAGEMENT

I exhale fully as I feel the last twitches of Jalen's cock as he finishes coming. I'm still facing away from him, and I leave his cock inside me for a moment.

"Oh wow." His voice is shaky. "That was so *hot*."

"I would've shown my stories to you a lot sooner," I whispered between gasps, "if I had known *that* was how you would react."

"What?" Jalen runs his fingertips down my sides. "How did you think I'd react?"

"Honestly? I was worried you'd laugh at me. Or you'd be, I don't know, insulted."

"Why would I be insulted?"

"Because—because I'm writing about you doing all these dirty, nasty things to me in my stories, but we haven't exactly been, uh...." I look at the floor. "...intimate much lately."

"What do you mean? We're plenty—"

I twist my body and look at Jalen. "That's the first time we've had sex in three months, Jalen."

His mouth falls open. "No way, it hasn't been that long."

"I'm afraid it has."

"Why haven't we—"

"Your travel schedule, babe." I pat his knee and start to stand. His cock slips out of me, along with a good dollop of his jizz. It splashes on his thigh, but he doesn't seem to notice.

"My travel schedule? But it's just for a couple of weeks."

"Every month. And then you have to reacclimate to the time change, and then you have to work late in the office. It just never happened."

"But that's just been the last two times I've been home. It hasn't been two months."

I tilt my head as I grab a tissue, then bend forward and wipe off the glob of cum from his leg. "You want me to get a calendar? It has, in fact, been three months. More, actually. Fourteen weeks."

Jalen smiles wistfully. "But who's counting, right?"

I kneel down next to the chair. "Jalen, I *love* being with you. I love it when you make love to me and treat me like a princess, and I love it when you fuck me and treat me like a dirty whore. I can't go on *not* having sex with you for months at a time. I'll go crazy." I shake my head. "And now, that bitch Alicia Parker is your boss, and she's never forgotten that I was the first girl you asked out after breaking up with her. Even though she's married with kids now. She's still pissed off about it."

Jalen sighs. "I know. She told me I'd have to step up my game if I want to keep my job."

"Step up your game? You've hit your numbers for the last six quarters! You were the top salesperson in the company last year!"

"And now," Jalen mumbled, frowning, "it's a new company, and Alicia will treat me like shit."

"Can you get a new job?"

"I'll start looking as soon as I can, babe, but Alicia is sending me back to Zurich next week."

"Next week? But you just got home!"

"I can still apply for jobs from Zurich."

The rage I'd been suppressing since I ran into Alicia at the coffee shop boils over. I seethe, my fists opening and closing at my sides. "This is personal, Jalen. She can't do this."

He shrugs. "I know it's not fair, but I asked around. She's a star at Beckett Equity. She isn't going anywhere. She could run over the CEO's daughter with her car and not get fired."

"God, I'm so *fucking* pissed off at her." I stomp around the room, wearing just the chemise, my boobs jiggling with each step. "I want to tear her limb from limb. Show her what a *real* woman can do to defend herself. I always let her walk all over me in high school. She used to knock the books out of my hands and call me a whore. I won't put up with it anymore, Jalen."

I look over at him. His pants are still down around his ankles, but the look on his face is almost starstruck. His cock is standing at attention.

"You're hard again already?"

"I—uh, yeah, I guess I am." He smiles crookedly.

"Why?" I put my hands on my hips.

"You're all fired up. Your breasts are totally falling out of your nightie."

"Chemise."

"And you're talking about getting into a fight with my ex over me."

I scoff and fold my arms. "Oh, now catfights are hot?"

"I don't know that I actually want to see you throw any punches, but I like you all wound up like this."

"Jalen, come on. This is goddamn serious. That bitch could totally fuck up our life. *If* she hasn't already. I won't take another minute of her bullshit."

Jalen stands up and kicks his way out of his suit pants and then takes off his tie and starts unbuttoning his shirt. "Get on your hands and knees, Rachel."

"I'm being serious. I'll punch that bitch in the face the next time I see her."

"Yeah," Jalen murmured, pulling off his socks.

"I won't let her destroy everything we've worked for just because she's jealous that she didn't get to fuck you. And I *won't* have you distracting me with your cock."

He closed the distance to me in two steps. "Keep talking. What else will you do to Alicia when you confront her?" he asked. "But tell me when I'm fucking you from behind."

Half of me wanted to scream obscenities at Jalen, to tell him that this was a massive threat to our relationship and not to take it so lightly.

Maybe that half would have won if I'd been fucked properly in the last two months. Yes, my orgasm was incredible while I was sitting in Jalen's lap, impaled on his cock while I read aloud, between moans, the filthy things Jeff was doing to Dr. Bennet. But I hadn't been fucked from behind for months—more than three, maybe even more than six. Suddenly I found myself on my hands and knees on the floor of the office, my chemise gathered around my waist.

Jalen slapped the right cheek of my bare ass, once, then twice. "You gonna hunt that bitch down, or make her come to you?"

I flinch slightly with each smack, but I didn't give anything away in my voice. "Hunt that bitch down."

"Yeah?" Another smack.

"Yeah. There's a coffee shop she hangs out in downtown. I'll go there and give her a piece of my mind."

"Yeah? What'll you do at the coffee shop?"

"She goes at the same time every day and gets some obnoxious drink. All the baristas roll their eyes when she walks in." He smacks my ass again, this time on the left cheek, and I inhale sharply. "I'm gonna knock her drink out of her hand like she used to with my books. Hit it *toward* her, so she gets espresso and whipped cream and all that no-sugar-flavored hazelnut shit all over her Dolce & Gabbana suit."

"What will you say to her?"

"I'll pick her up by the lapels of her three-thousand-dollar silk blazer and slam her into the wall. I'll tell her she can't keep sending you away for two weeks at a time. I'll knock her damn teeth out."

Jalen kneels behind me, and runs both his hands lovingly over my ass. "Say that again."

"I'll knock her fucking teeth out." God, my beautiful husband is behind me, touching me, with his whole hand, so that I feel the rough skin patches on his fingers and palms. I can't help but think that I wouldn't have gotten this man—this cut, well-hung guy; the guy with the hard, taut stomach; the broad shoulders and the kind eyes; the most attractive guy at my high school; the star athlete every girl wanted to bed in college—without my body just the way it is.

"Alicia told me I have to do a whole European tour," he says. Then he leans over my body, his muscular chest touching my back, and whispers in my ear, "She wants me to be away from you for six weeks next time."

I grit my teeth. I don't know if Jalen is telling the truth, or if he's just saying it to get me angry and horny, but whatever—it's working. My pussy is begging for it again. I'd just been fucked crazy good, but my adrenaline is pumping through my veins now, and his cock, still wet with my juices, lightly touches my right ass cheek, about three inches south of where he'd spanked me. "She can't do that to my man."

When the words "my man" leave my mouth, I feel his cock twitch and I hear him breathe in quickly. "Yes, that's right. Say that again, baby."

"She can't do that to my man."

A low moan escapes from him. "Who am I?"

"You're my man, Jalen. You're fucking *mine*. You don't belong to that bitch, you belong to *me*. And I'll make sure that bitch knows you're my man."

Jalen slips his tantalizing dick inside me and I moan.

"What am I?"

"You're my man."

"Say it again."

"You're my man."

"Keep fucking saying it, Rachel."

"You belong to me, Jalen. No one else gets that dick but me. Keep giving that big cock to me."

"Oh yeah, Rachel. Beg for it."

"I'm not going to beg for it, you dirty boy. That cock is mine. I own it. You fucking belong to me."

"Oh, holy fuck, Rachel." His pumping inside my pussy quickened. He was still bent over me, his breath hot and urgent in my ear. "That's right, baby."

"She keeps calling me a dirty whore, but I'm the dirty whore who's fucking the man she wants to fuck." I moan. "She cries every time her husband fucks her with his tiny little cock because she wishes it were you. She doesn't even know what a phenomenal dick you have, Jalen. Oh—oh, right there, keep doing that, *shit*."

Jalen straightens up slightly and he's getting one particular spot inside me perfectly.

My arms can't hold me up any more, and I sink down, my face and my shoulders against the soft carpet—which only improves the angle. My breath becomes more ragged, even as I become aware that I still need to keep up my dirty talk. "She can't even *fantasize* about how good your cock is." I moan louder. "That's how much she doesn't know. That's how much she settled for when she couldn't have you. She can't even imagine how good you are, Jalen."

"Tell me you need me," he says softly.

"I fucking need you and your big cock," I say. The sensations are too much. I'm going to come again, really soon.

"Tell me one more time."

"I—I—love you, Jalen," I gasp, and then my orgasm hits, even more powerful than last time. I feel the muscles of my vagina contract over and over, pulsing against his cock as he slides in and out of my pussy, and then he groans, low and loud and feral, and then he's coming inside me.

I'm vaguely aware than my right leg has started to shake

slightly, and I try to get it to stop, but with Jalen holding my ass at this angle while he empties his seed inside me, I can't do anything about it. I don't know what noises I'm making, I just know I can't be without him for two more weeks, never mind six.

I try to focus on my breathing until the world slips back to being right side up and the room stops spinning.

Shit. Did I just say all that stuff about him belonging to me? That's—that's really weird and dirty, and I don't know if he's okay with that.

"Oooh," I manage to squeak out, and Jalen slides out of my pussy, this time with gravity keeping his cum inside me. "Was—was that okay?"

"Was that okay? Holy shit, Rachel, that was the fucking hottest sex I've ever had. If I didn't go crazy being away from you for two weeks, I'd suggest we stay away from each other for just as long next time."

"Absence makes the dick get harder?" I smile, my face in the carpet.

"Something like that, yeah."

I clear my throat. "It was okay? The stuff about, you know, you belonging to me and stuff like that?"

He laughs. "I've never been so turned on. You completely submitting to me, face down on the floor, while you're moaning about beating up my ex-girlfriend and telling me I belong to you." He shudders. "Yeah, you'll have to do that again."

"Again?" I say incredulously.

He chuckles. "Well, maybe later tonight."

I push myself up to a kneeling position, feeling his hot

cum drip out of my vagina. "Can we—can we just go to bed? I want us to sleep naked together. I miss you holding me."

He steps around in front of me and puts his hands out, palms up. I place my hands in his and he helps me get to my feet. "Definitely. I've missed holding you, too." He smirks. "Seriously, after a couple of months without making love to you, I'm pretty sure I'll want to do stuff with you if you sleep in the nude."

"It's a chance I'm willing to take," I deadpan.

Fifteen minutes later, my makeup off and his suit hung carefully in the closet, he and I are wrapped up in bed together, with my head on his shoulder and my leg draped over his. He reaches over and switches off the bedside lamp, and it's dark and cool in our bedroom, with only the light of full moon coming in the window to illuminate our bodies.

I breathe in and out slowly. It's not that late—it's not even eleven—but I'm exhausted. Not just from the two rounds of hot, urgent sex we just had, but the two months of doubt I've gone through, the stress his travel has put on me, and the anger at Alicia.

I've got to let that shit go.

THE BEST DEFENSE

One of the nice things about my job is that—when Jalen is home—he and I work about six blocks from each other. Sometimes we commute together, although his hours are often much longer than mine. But even when we don't drive in the same car, we can meet for lunch or coffee in the afternoon.

I wake up briefly at a quarter to five, the two of us still tangled in each other's naked bodies. I'm safe and warm. Jalen finally feels like he's home, like he's come back to me. I fall asleep again quickly.

I open my eyes again at six fifteen, and I'm still resting my head on Jalen's chest. He places soft, gentle kisses on the top of my head.

"Good morning," I murmur, my voice thick with sleep.

"Hello, beautiful." He entwines his fingers in my hair and then twirls his hand until it comes free. "I don't really want to go to work today."

"Me neither. Maybe we could play hooky and just spend the day in bed."

Jalen sighs. "As wonderful as that sounds, I'd have hell to pay when I went back in. It would seem like I'm avoiding Alicia."

"You could update your résumé."

He laughs. "That's why I sat down at the computer in the first place. Then I got distracted by some scorching, sexy story about me and some hot, curvy doctor."

"If you stay in bed and call in sick, I'll give you a blow job. Then I'll cook breakfast for you naked."

"Dammit, Rachel, I'm not strong enough to deal with that kind of temptation."

I kiss my way down his chest to his stomach. He's still unclothed and I see, out of the corner of my eye, his cock stiffening.

His phone rings on the bedside table.

"Don't get it," I say between kisses.

"It's Alicia. Perfect time for me to tell her I'm not coming in today."

"What the hell is she calling you at a quarter after six for?" I look up at him, hoping he'll get off the phone quickly so I can continue my journey south.

"Hell if I know." He answers, making his voice gravelly. "Hi, Alicia. I'm glad you called. I'm not feeling well—"

Then he stops and listens. He purses his lips. "No, that's not right. That deal was supposed to be closed. The deal *was* closed. Why did you—"

More talking on the other end. I can't make out what she's saying, but Jalen's face grows tighter, his eyes narrowing.

"I haven't even officially reported to you for twenty-four hours yet, and already you've screwed up a closed deal?"

I wince. She might be his ex, but I'm not sure he should be talking to his boss like that.

"Hey—hold on, Alicia. That document was signed before the company acquisition became official. You can't just rescind it."

I clearly hear Alicia's voice on the other end say, "I just did."

Jalen raises his voice. "I worked on that deal for *months*. Did you purposely screw it up so that I'd have to travel to Zurich tomorrow? Is this because—" He pauses. "Hello? Alicia?" He takes the phone away from his face and looks at the screen. "She hung up on me."

"Sorry."

He puts his hand over his face. "So much for calling in sick today. I've got to go save the deal I closed last week. Alicia pulled it, saying the purchase order doesn't meet Beckett standards. She's got me on a flight to Zurich *tomorrow*."

I set my jaw. "I guess this means you can't get away for lunch, either."

"Even if I could, you better believe I'll be working on my résumé." He slides out of bed, and walks into the bathroom.

The shower turns on and the door closes.

Fuck. He's about to get on a plane and be gone for another two weeks. Alicia will try to break us up.

You know, Dr. Rachel Bennet would never put up with this shit.

I sit up on the edge of the bed and think for a few minutes.

I recall my conversation with Alicia at the Temple Coffee on 25th and H.

You could set your watch by my ten-o'clock extra-large half-caf quad latte.

I pick up my cell phone and call my boss's extension at work. I don't expect her in this early, so I leave a voicemail. "Hey, this is Rachel. I'm sorry, but I forgot I have an appointment this morning. I'll be in after lunch."

Five minutes later, Jalen rushes out of the bathroom naked. I look him up and down—he's so beautiful.

"Are you sure you don't want to stay home today?" I ask in my breathiest voice.

"I'm sure I *do* want to stay home today," Jalen says as he pulls a pair of boxer briefs out of his dresser drawer. "But we're talking a six-figure commission that my new boss purposely screwed up, and I'll have to make it right with the customer."

I watch him get dressed, pulling the shorts up over his tight, muscular ass, so perfect I want to bite it. Some of his former college athlete friends have filled out considerably, but Jalen is still lean. I admire the shape of his body as he walks to the closet and pulls out a light blue dress shirt.

"I'm sorry you have to go through this," I say, although the gears in my mind are churning.

"I'm sorry *you* have to go through this," Jalen says, buttoning the cuffs of his sleeves. "I shouldn't be jetting off to Europe so often when we're trying to start a family. I should have stopped this months ago." He takes a navy suit off the hanger and pulls his pants on.

"I like that suit on you."

He smiles. "You're just saying that because you want to get in my pants."

"Maybe." I can't help it. I was so low just a couple of days ago, but now, even though I know he's scheduled to leave again, being in the room with him, still in the faint afterglow of our lovemaking, has put everything right again for the time being.

And besides that, I have a plan forming in my head. "Text me if you're free for coffee this afternoon."

"If I've saved this deal by the afternoon, it'll be a miracle."

Dressed, he comes over to the bed, leans over, and kisses me on the mouth. I'm still naked, and I grab his hand and put it on my hip. The kiss goes on for a moment as he puts the other hand on the back of my head and opens his mouth. When he breaks from the kiss, he murmurs, "I really have to go."

"See you later."

"I love you, Rachel."

"I love you, too."

He turns and leaves the room. His footsteps go down the hall and then the front door opens and closes. There's the faint sound of an engine starting, then idling, then fading down the street.

I grab my phone again, and I search for an app that lets me record video directly to cloud storage. I go into the closet and pull all my purses out. One by one I put them on the bed, finding the ones with high inside pockets, and stick my smartphone in each, seeing how far over the top of the purse they stick out. I do a couple of test recordings, and I figure out how to start and stop the recording through my Bluetooth earbuds. The audio isn't top quality, especially if I'm standing across the room, but you can still easily make out what I'm saying.

THE BEST DEFENSE | 209

I go to my laptop and search online for legal precedents. This is a little trickier, as California law isn't really on my side on this one, but there are a few things I can do to make sure I cover myself.

I look at the clock. I have more than enough time to get ready and establish myself at Temple Coffee. And I'm counting on being able to push Alicia's buttons again.

I almost forgot I needed a bag for my laptop and I had to search through my closet, but I found my chic beige-and-brown satchel under a pile of sweaters. I try to keep myself calm on the drive downtown, and I enter Temple Coffee at a few minutes before ten.

After I order my simple café au lait, I tell the barista I'm an author—which is kind of true—and ask if I can record my video blog in the café. "My followers would love to see where I get my inspiration."

"Knock yourself out," the barista says, clearly uninterested.

I plunk myself down in a chair with an excellent view of the front door. I dig my phone out and put it in the top inside pocket of my purse, so just the camera is sticking out of the top. Then I carefully set my purse on the table, just behind my laptop. There are a few other people scattered at tables around the coffee shop, but none near where I'm sitting. If it stays this way, I'll know the universe is on my side.

"Oh, neat," the barista says, making me jump. I didn't notice her bringing my coffee over in a porcelain cup with a saucer. There's a beautiful rosette design in the steamed milk. "That's clever—using your purse as the camera stand. You said you're an author?"

"Yep. Working on my website today."

"Right."

"That's a fantastic design. I've never seen a rosette before. You do this?"

She nods. "I'm a fine arts major at Sac IAD. I paint, but my latte art is getting better too."

I look at her nametag, which says *Charlotte*. "Oh, neat. You have a website too?"

She laughs. "No, but now I think I should make one."

"You paint under your real name? Charlotte...."

"Char, actually. Char Davies. Yeah, for now, I paint under my real name."

"A student art show, maybe?"

She smiles. "I have to be accepted first, but keep asking. I'll know in about a month."

"Great. Nice to meet, you, Char."

The barista turns and leaves. I look at the clock on my screen. I have about ten minutes before Alicia's daily visit.

So I get everything set up. I have a blog program open in front of me, and I even type a few lines about how I'm excited to start my next book. It's just for show, but it looks real enough. I reach over to the phone and boot up the app, making sure the camera is pointed both at the chair in front of me and at the front door.

The countdown is at two minutes, and I push the button on my Bluetooth earbuds that starts the recording session.

"Here I am, author Rachel Jefferson, at one of my favorite hangouts, the Temple Coffee on 25th and H Streets, here in beautiful downtown Sacramento, the city I've called my home for the last two years."

I continue to ramble, making stuff up as I go along, my eyes trained like a hawk on the front doors.

At 10 AM—on the dot, just like she said—I see Alicia through the outside windows.

I look over at the barista. She blanches, and immediately starts grinding beans.

Alicia opens the door and steps toward the counter, but then she sees me, talking, and does a double-take. "The usual, Christina," she says loudly and then walks up to my table.

"Hang up," she says.

"I'm not on the phone."

"Like hell you aren't. I said, hang up."

I put my hand to my ear, but I don't touch the button. "Okay," I say, "now that you've interrupted me, what do you want? You seem to be hell-bent on taking my husband away from me."

Alicia smiles, a condescending grin that shows her upper gums. "Now you'll feel the same humiliation I felt, Rachel. The long, lonely nights when I was sure he was cheating on me with someone else. And all the shit I went through when everyone found out he dumped me for a girl who wasn't even pretty."

I nod. "Seems like professional suicide to me, Alicia."

"Oh, don't you worry about me. I'll make everything look like his fault. I already logged in as him, from the office, and sent his precious customer an email rescinding that big deal he closed last week. He'll be in Zurich for a month cleaning that up." She laughs. "I'll make his life hell. And there's *no way* he'll get that commission."

"Seriously, Alicia, I didn't do anything to you in high school to steal Jalen from you. He didn't even ask me out until the two of you broke up. And besides, it's been over fifteen years. Don't you have a great life now? Husband, two kids, great job, all that? Can't you just ignore me at holiday parties or something?"

"Fuck you, Rachel. And fuck Jalen too. When we come back from Zurich—after we find that there's just one room in their sold-out hotel for us to share, by the way—I'll talk to every financial services company in Sacramento and tell them that he can't be trusted. I know Beckett like the back of my hand. Trust me, *no one* will suspect I'm responsible for anything. And I'll make you wonder, every night that he's away from home, if he's fucking me senseless. The way that I wondered about you. Except you know I *am* pretty. You know that guys line themselves up to get next to me. How long will Jalen be able to hold out?" She giggles. "It'll be delicious. And that giant ass and those big tits won't bail you out this time."

"So you won't stop until you ruin our lives?"

"That's right."

"And all because he asked me out after the two of you broke up our senior year of high school."

She shakes her head. "Don't play innocent with me. I know you had your eye on him for years. I know you were jealous of me."

"What if I go to your boss?"

"Monty?" She seethes. "I've got him wrapped around my little finger. That disgusting weasel thinks if he plays his cards right, he can get in my pants. But all I have to do is bat my eyelashes at him, show him some leg, and deny everything. There's no paper trail. Besides, who is Monty going to believe? Me, the woman who's been at his right hand for six years, or you, his incompetent employee's crazy wife?"

I narrow my eyes. "Maybe you should get out of here, Alicia."

"Maybe *you* should get out of here," she says. "This is *my* goddamn coffee shop, not yours. Don't come in here ever again. Not unless you want me calling the director of the State Infrastructure Office to get *your* fat ass fired."

"Is that a threat?"

"It's a promise."

Closing my laptop, I put it in its case, put the straps of the satchel and my purse over my shoulder, and, avoiding eye contact with Alicia, grab my mostly full café au lait and head up to the counter.

Char sets down the extra-large paper cup with Alicia's complicated latte. "You need that to go?"

I nod.

Char leans forward and lowers her voice. "You got that all on video, didn't you?"

I nod again.

"Hang on," she says, more loudly. "These cups seem damaged. We have some more in the back."

I hear Alicia audibly sigh. Char comes back less than thirty seconds later—though with Alicia behind me, and me wondering if I'll get caught, it seems like much longer. "Here," she whispers, sliding a paper over to me. "This is a form to shoot video in the store. We got a few when the news team did the feature on our charity work last month. I signed the bottom. Fill it out when you get home and make sure you have this if Little-Miss-Can't-Let-It-Go over there bitches at you about right to privacy." She expertly pours my café au lait into the to-go cup without spilling a drop. "And if you need someone to back up what she said, you just let me know."

"Is my latte ready yet, Christina?" Alicia asks. I see Char flinch at *Christina*.

"It's right here, ma'am." She picks up the cup, and as she walks toward Alicia, who is now sitting at the table I just vacated, she says under her breath, "With a special surprise ingredient, on the house."

I turn my back to Alicia so she can't see my grin. I put the paper in my satchel, next to my laptop, tap my earbuds to stop recording, and then walk out the door.

"Oh, and Rachel?" Alicia calls after me, but I don't turn around. I wouldn't be able to suppress my giggles.

THE BOSS'S OFFICE

I've been back in my office for about two hours. My stomach is starting to complain, but after the emails I sent when I got in—including a little proactive explaining to my boss about potential calls she might get—I was behind. I'd probably need to stay late one or two nights this week, but I hoped it would be worth it.

The phone on my desk rang. It was Jalen's work number. I hoped it was Jalen, but I suppose it could have been Alicia, telling me that she'd figured out my plan and put a stop to it. I closed my eyes, my heart beating fast, and picked up the receiver.

"Rachel Jefferson."

"Rachel, it's Zack Montgomery from Beckett Equity."

"Oh—hello, Mr. Montgomery. You're, uh, Jalen's manager's manager, if I'm not mistaken."

"You're not mistaken." He clears his throat. "I wanted to make sure that you were the sender of the email that came into my inbox about ninety minutes ago."

"Yes, sir," I say. "I sent a video to you."

"There's no need for the formality," he says gruffly. "My friends call me Monty. Although I suspect you already knew that from the video."

"That's correct."

There is silence on the other end of the line for a moment.

"Monty? Are you still there?"

"What do you want, Rachel?"

"What do I want? I want my husband home for more than half the month, I want his commission in our account, and I want him to stop reporting to a woman who wants him and me financially ruined."

There's silence, but only for a brief moment. "Would you come over to my office this afternoon? Maybe just before five o'clock? Your husband still works in the Woodward Reynolds building. We haven't consolidated yet, but maybe you can meet him afterward and go out for a nice dinner."

"That sounds lovely."

I hang up. Zack Montgomery didn't give anything away on the phone. I wonder if I'll need the film rights form that Charlotte gave me after all.

At 4:41 PM, I walk into the Beckett Equity building. The black marble and light gray granite is sterile and imposing. As I take the elevator up to the eleventh floor, I break into a light sweat. Maybe this wasn't such a great idea. I could be met with threats of a lawsuit or a gaggle of lawyers. Alicia could be waiting for me with a two-by-four with a nail in it for all I know.

The elevator doors open, and there's no one waiting there to beat me up. A young white guy behind the reception desk walks me over to Monty's office. As I pass between the low cubicles, I look around, and from about twenty yards away, I see Alicia in an office of her own on the phone. She looks up, drops the phone, and runs toward me as fast as her Louboutin heels can carry her. "Fred—Fred—what are you doing? What's she doing here?"

"It's *Frank,* Ms. Hawthorne, and this woman is here at Monty's request."

Alicia shoots daggers at me with her eyes and then falls into step with us, right up behind me in my personal space. "It won't work, you whore," she hisses into my ear. Her breath is unpleasant but I don't flinch, and I keep walking. My stomach is doing somersaults, but the last thing I want to show Alicia is how nervous I am.

Frank opens the door to Monty's office. A white man with short salt-and-pepper hair, a matching Van Dyke, and a smart black pinstriped suit, is sitting behind his mahogany desk, his laptop open in front of him.

Frank speaks first. "Rachel Jefferson is here to see—"

Alicia pushes ahead of Frank, and he catches himself against the doorjamb. "I don't know what she told you, Monty, but just because she's upset about her husband's recent screw-ups doesn't mean—"

Monty presses a key on the laptop, and Alicia's voice, tinny, seething with anger, is audible.

"Monty? I've got him wrapped around my little finger. That disgusting weasel thinks if he plays his cards right, he can get in my pants. But all I have to do is bat my eyelashes at him, show him some

leg, and deny everything. There's no paper trail. Besides, who is Monty going to believe—"

He clicks the audio off.

Alicia's mouth opens and closes, like a fish.

Monty taps the fingers of his left hand on the desk in front of him. "I've worked with you for six years now, Alicia, and you're talented. I've even said you're the future of this company. I've gone to bat for you a few times, I don't mind telling you."

"I—it was taken out of context, Monty."

He shakes his head. "You have disappointed me on many levels, Alicia. Not the least of which is that you didn't cover your tracks."

The color drains out of Alicia's face, and it's all I can do to keep still and register no emotion on my face.

Monty turns to me. "Mr. Jefferson will have his full commission for this sale in his bank account at the close of business today. He no longer has to travel to Zurich tomorrow. Instead, *I'll* be meeting in person with the client." His eyes dart to Alicia. "It's all very inconvenient to have to travel internationally on a moment's notice," he says. "My wife isn't too pleased with me. Of course, your trip has been canceled too, Alicia. I'd prefer you clean up the mess you made, but I'm not sure I can trust you to do that."

Frank clears his throat.

"Ah, yes," Monty says. "I apologize for all of this, Frank. Would you escort Ms. Hawthorne back to her office?"

"No, Monty, that's not necessary, I need to tell my side—"

"You'll have an opportunity, Ms. Hawthorne, but it is not today. I suggest you collect your things and prepare yourself for a week or two off. Without corporate access. I haven't decided what the appropriate course of action is, but you shouldn't be in the building for a while."

Alicia gulps and nods.

"I need to talk to Ms. Jefferson," he says.

She closes her eyes and murmurs, "Allan will be so mad at me."

Monty sets his jaw. "Frank, please close the door on your way out."

Frank and Alicia back out of the office, and I step forward and take a seat in a guest chair in front of the desk.

"I know my lawyers say to never apologize for anything," he begins, "but to hell with that. Forget about what kind of liability she just opened us up to—what she did to you is unconscionable." He leans forward, but stares off to the side. "I'm deeply sorry for her actions. I'll do everything I can to make it right. Your husband was one of Woodward Reynolds' top salespeople, and it's not hard to see why. We're making it very difficult for him to stay. I'll have to consider how I can fix this." He looks in my eyes. "You'll give me a chance to make up for it?"

I hesitate. "Look, uh, Monty, she's only been his boss for less than a week. I didn't have any agenda about taking you to court. I haven't contacted a lawyer about this. I was just recording my video blog in a coffee shop when she threatened me and my livelihood. And she mentioned your name—it wasn't too hard to find you online—and I thought you'd want to know, and I thought you could put a stop to it."

"Consider it stopped," he said. "Okay, it's past five o'clock, and that's enough of this for one day. You know La Table Royale?"

"Uh... yeah. There's only a six-month waiting list to get in."

"Not for Zack Montgomery. If you want it, you and your husband have a six o'clock reservation there. A little early, perhaps, but it *was* short notice."

My jaw drops. "Absolutely!" With the commission check showing up in our account tonight, we can definitely afford it, as pricey as it is.

"I've also reviewed your husband's travel schedule the last few months, and I believe he deserves to take the rest of the week off, no vacation time needed. It won't make up for *all* those missed weekends, but it's a start."

I wonder if my boss will let me take a couple of vacation days too.

He stands. "Now, Ms. Jefferson, I need to make some travel arrangements. I may be in touch in the next few days with a couple of ideas on how to make this right."

PRICE FIXE

I had just enough time to go home, change clothes, and put on makeup. I didn't have any time to debate with myself for an hour over what dress to wear. I knew I wanted to be sexy for Jalen, so I took out a low-cut red minidress. It's one that in the past I'd been a little self-conscious to wear, but tonight I'd gotten the better of Alicia Parker Hawthorne, and I wanted Jalen to screw me senseless after dinner. This was the dress to do the trick. Lots of cleavage, lots of thigh.

I find parking about two spots away from Jalen's car and I rush as fast as I can in my heels to La Table Royale. Jalen is waiting just inside the door, sitting in a straight-backed chair next to the maître-d's station. He's still in his dashingly handsome navy suit, the top button of his light blue dress shirt undone, tie askew and just so. He's the most handsome man in the restaurant, and I'm going home with him.

He stands and pulls me into a kiss. I wrap my arms around him. This is definitely a kiss we shouldn't be having in public, but I don't mind.

I break from the kiss first. "I was going to ask you if you were mad at me for being so late, but after that kiss, I guess you can't be too angry."

"What are you talking about? You're not even five minutes late. The maître-d' isn't even here." He takes a step back and looks me up and down. "I was very impressed, catching Alicia like that," he says. "You saved my job—"

"—and maybe even our marriage," I cut in.

He nods. "And you still had time to go home and get dressed up."

"I was in jeans. I'd have felt uncomfortable coming here."

"Well, now *I'm* underdressed. *I* should have been the one to take care of the situation."

I shake my head. "She had all the power because of your work situation. And I still had some power over her because she hates me so much that she can't think straight around me. She kept running her mouth off. If she'd just shut up about her diabolical plans for world domination, she might be on that flight to Zurich with you tomorrow morning."

"Things certainly changed after lunch," he said. "I got a couple of cryptic emails, first from accounting, stating that my commission check would be deposit in our account at the end of the day and then from our travel agency, telling me that I'd been taken off the flight to Zurich and that I didn't need to reschedule. For a second, I thought I was in big trouble. But then I remembered the look in your eyes I saw when I left this morning. You had something planned, didn't you?"

I fake my best southern accent. "Who, li'l ol' me?"

The maître-d' arrives and asks us if we have a reservation.

"Six o'clock," I say. "It's under *Monty*."

"Ah, yes," she says, nodding. "Mr. Montgomery called earlier about this. I can take you now."

We follow her to a table in the back, with high-backed booths in reddish-brown leather. The white tablecloth contrasts with the colorful red, orange, and purple floral centerpiece. Each of the white cloth napkins are folded into a bird shape. The whole table is beautiful, like something out of a period drama.

Jalen and I sit across from each other and the maître-d' hands us the menus. La Table Royale is known for a constantly rotating *price fixe* menu, decadent and superb, and always has the whole valley raving. Tonight's menu features six courses that I can barely recognize, let alone pronounce.

A tuxedoed sommelier appears at our table with an ice bucket and a bottle of Champagne.

"Oh," I say, "we didn't order—"

"Compliments of Mr. Montgomery," the sommelier says as he opens the bottle with a pop. He expertly pours us both a glass in beautiful crystal flutes. "Enjoy."

I look across at Jalen. "Can you believe this?"

"All this and I *still* don't have to travel to Zurich tomorrow. Am I dreaming?"

I shake my head.

"And this is all because of you."

"Well," I say, "I couldn't have done it if Alicia hadn't been so petty and short-sighted."

"Shall we drink to Alicia?" He raises his glass.

I laugh. "Hell no. Let's drink to Monty, a businessperson who is actually fair and generous."

"To Monty." Jalen takes a swig.

My boss isn't thrilled about it, but she lets me take Thursday and Friday off. We wake up late on Thursday, and Jalen insists that right after a leisurely breakfast I read aloud to him again, with me in his lap. I start reading *The Princess and the Unicorn*, and after about twenty pages he again has his gorgeous cock pumping in and out of me while I writhe in his lap and try to keep reading without losing my place.

We spend the day lazing around, watching a couple of TV shows we didn't get around to, and then falling into sexual escapades. We watch one show with me laying my head in Jalen's lap, and when the closing credits roll, I pull his dick out and give him a slow, sensual blow job. A few hours later, right after Jalen makes us gin and tonics and we enjoy the sunshine on our back patio, he leads me by the hand to one of our lounge chairs where he proceeds to lift my skirt and pull my panties off. Then he performs tantalizing oral on me until I come, my juices are all over his face. Afterward, we walk hand in hand inside, where we make love on the sofa, me on top, grinding my clit into his body as he thrusts up inside me, and I come twice more before he finally orgasms, shooting his jizz inside me.

Jalen checks his email on his phone as we're lying on the sofa in the afterglow, and chuckles. "Damn, Rachel, you really put the fear of God into Monty. He's asking me for a meeting on Monday to discuss my goals for the upcoming year and where I see myself at Beckett Equity."

"Any mention of Alicia?" I blurt out before I can stop myself.

"Nope. Although she must be even more embarrassed

than her namesake nurse was in that werewolf story you wrote."

I start to blush. "I can't believe I was so scared to show those stories to you."

"You won't stop writing them, will you?"

"I don't know. I was pretty much doing it because I was so frustrated that you were gone all the time and I wasn't getting any."

"And now that I'm home and we're having sex three times a day, no more stories?"

I giggle. "You seem to like them. Especially when I put in some dirty parts that you and I haven't done before. I didn't know you were into some of that stuff."

"It's more that the thought of doing it with *you*, especially when it's getting you off, which is the real turn-on. I mean, I'm not into unicorns or anything, but if I'm a unicorn that you're sexually attracted to? Damn, I'll strap a rainbow horn to my forehead and whinny."

"Is anything too over-the-top? Like, I haven't written anything about orgies or key parties or anything."

"You're into orgies and key parties?"

"I'm not saying I am. I'm just asking you if I wrote it, if you'd want me to read it while I was sitting on your lap."

Jalen laughed. "If I'm fucking you in your story, I can almost guarantee I'll love it when you read it to me while you're sitting on my lap." He kissed my forehead. "You probably know I'm not into group sex, but reading about the two of us doing it—that's kind of a different thing."

The doorbell rings.

"You expecting anyone?" I ask, pushing myself up to my hands and knees.

He grins. "I was going to ask if you knew where the big bowl was for the key party."

I laugh, stand up and pull my skirt down, button my blouse back up and then assess myself. Jalen undid my bra when he came inside, and it's over by the leg of the dining room table. My panties are still in a wad outside. I hope the wind hasn't kicked up and blown them anywhere embarrassing. I haven't gone out in public without a bra since before I turned thirty, but I suppose receiving a delivery from UPS or something isn't all that bad.

Jalen is pulling his pants on, and as he zips up his fly, I walk to our front door and open it.

It's Alicia.

THE UPPER HAND

*A*licia stands on our front step with an absolutely terrified look on her face. She's dressed in a skin-tight, barely-there, caution-tape-yellow minidress. It conforms to her body so snugly I wonder if she's having trouble breathing. She's also in a pair of strappy gold stilettos, which look equally uncomfortable.

Her blonde hair is down, flowing in waves just past her shoulders, and her face is made up more heavily than I'm used to seeing her.

One more thing: there's a black leather dog collar around her neck. It's attached to a leash, and holding the other end of the leash is Alicia's husband, Allan, dressed in black slacks and a black dress shirt.

"Alicia?" I ask in disbelief.

"Who is it?" Jalen calls.

"It's, uh, Alicia," I call back, "and her husband."

"Hello, again," Allan says pleasantly. "I must apologize for just showing up out of the blue like this, but I'm sorry to say that Alicia didn't leave me much choice."

"What's with the leash?" I ask, and immediately bite my tongue. I don't want to know.

"That's not important," Allan says, waving his hand at me. "What *is* important is that my wife has something she must ask you."

Jalen's footsteps sound on the floor behind me. I turn and see him, still shirtless, as he steps into the entry. "Did you say it was *Alicia*—" He stops talking as soon as he catches sight of Alicia's face. "What's going on? Why are you here?" Then he gets closer and sees Allan. And sees Allan holding the leash. "What the hell is going on?"

"I don't know, Jalen. Allan was just about to explain it to me." I lift my hand for him to continue.

"I'm very upset with Alicia for the cruel things she's done to the two of you this week," he says. "Not only did she intend to jeopardize your relationship, she intended to cheat on me, and I can't have that."

"I've been a naughty girl," Alicia says.

Allan scoffs. "That's not the worst part. If my father hadn't pulled some strings, she'd be fired now, and we need her paycheck. If it were just the two of us, that would be one thing, but with one paycheck and two kids, it was undeniably irresponsible."

"She won't be my boss anymore, will she?" Jalen asks sharply.

"Not on your life," Allan says. His lip curls slightly. "You, my friend, are far too tempting for her to be around." He looks at me, up and down, and I'm a little nervous that I don't have my bra and panties on. "Aha," he says. Then he turns to Alicia. "I don't know what your problem is, Alicia. Rachel is beautiful. In a different way than you are, but she *is* beautiful. I insist that you stop this."

Alicia blushes deeply. "I—I can't."

"You'll have to learn," Allan says sharply. "Listen, I don't want to stand here with the door open. Especially when I'm holding my wife on a leash. May we come in?"

"Uh...."

Allan holds up his hands. "Alicia is under control. No yelling, no violence, no insults. You have my word."

As much as I don't like the idea of Alicia in my house, this whole situation has me curious. She won't attack me— or at least, I'm pretty sure she won't. Not with her husband here.

I have to admit that I know precious little about the kind of relationships where one person finds themselves in a slutty dress and stilettos in public on the end of a leash. Thinking of myself in the skintight dress and the collar and Jalen holding the lead makes a shiver run up my spine—in a good way. I know Jalen and I just finished our second full-body-contact lovemaking session of the day, but the heat turns up under me again. I take a step back into the entry-way. "Just for a minute."

Jalen steps forward, right behind me. "Wait—Rachel, you don't—"

"It's just for a minute, Jalen."

The two of them step inside the entryway and shut the door behind them.

"Well, Alicia?" Allan says, firmly but not unkindly. "Don't you have something you want to ask them?"

"I—" Alicia starts and then gulps and takes a couple of deep breaths. "I've never stopped thinking about the two of you together. Not since you asked her out in high school, Jalen. Not when you were my boyfriend again, not after I left to go to college, not when I was in relationships with other guys." She winces. "Not even when I married Allan."

"Alicia," Jalen begins, but she cuts him off.

"No—it's not that I couldn't get *you* out of my head, Jalen. I couldn't get *the two of you* out of my head. I have these vivid dreams where the two of you are fucking, and you're both in ecstasy. Sometimes, if it's a good dream, you'll let him come in your mouth, Rachel, and then you'll turn to me and tell me that *I* never let him do that."

I blink hard. "Uh, no. I can honestly say I never realized you were thinking anything even remotely like that."

"Other times the two of you are in bed, the covers pulled up, but the way you're moving and the way you're looking at each other—I know you're making love. You turn your head toward me, Rachel, and you say, 'How come Jalen never looked at *you* like that? You're the one with the size-2 dresses and the long legs and the perfect, white teeth, so what's wrong with you that he broke up with you for me?'" Her breath hitches.

This is more along the lines of what I'd expect for Alicia: wanting everything in the world for herself, and completely insecure when anyone makes a choice that doesn't involve her.

"So," she continues haltingly, "what I really want is to *watch* the two of you."

I look in Alicia's eyes.

She's completely serious.

I glance at Allan. His arms are folded, though he's still holding the leash.

"I want to watch Jalen's face as you strip in front of him." Alicia rotates her hips slightly. She doesn't even seem to know she's doing it. "I want to see the raw, naked lust in his eyes when he sees you. I want the two of you to get into each other, touch each other, do the things you do when no one else is around." She raises her hand to her mouth and lightly bites her index finger. "And I want to see you both come. Completely let loose."

Jalen rests his hand on my upper arm. "Wow, that's a little bit fucked up," he whispers in my ear.

"It's a *lot* fucked up," I murmur, low enough that they can't hear us.

"Okay, I'll get them out of here." Jalen takes a step forward.

I put my hand firmly on his chest. He looks down at me, confusion crossing his face.

"I—I might want to."

Jalen's eyes widen. "You might want to *what?* Fuck in front of them?"

"Um," I stutter, "um, yeah. It's kinda hot."

Jalen tenses.

I lean back into him, feeling his naked pecs against my shoulder, the top of my ass at his crotch, his breath hot and quick on the back of my neck. "Think about it, Jalen. She's been fucking up our relationship since it started. Our first date got totally messed up because she kept looming over us. Even in college when we finally started sleeping together, we didn't get serious because of that first awkward date. And now that we've built a life together, she's here, trying to screw it up again."

"And now you want to fuck in front of her?"

I wiggle my ass, and he starts to stiffen. "You do too. You want to see the look on her face when you come inside me after I've orgasmed, when she knows for sure she can't have what's right in front of her."

"Oh my God, Rachel," he says, his breath quickening, "that's *all kinds* of wrong."

I reach down and run my hand right behind my ass, up his crotch, confirming that his cock is straining the fly of his jeans. "Wrong in the best way," I say. "Look at you. You're hard." I lean forward. "And I didn't put my panties back on."

Jalen looks up at Alicia and holds a finger up in warning. "Just watching. You can't touch me. Or her. That goes for you too." He nods at Allan.

"Maybe Allan can—" Alicia begins. Allan yanks the leash, not hard, but enough to get Alicia to stop talking.

"You won't do anything but watch them make love and think about what a bad person you are," Allan says to her, quietly. "We can discuss next steps after we get home."

"Yes, sir," Alicia says, firmly but with a note of misery in her voice.

"You sure you want to do this, Rachel?" Jalen asks softly.

"It'll be good fodder for my next story." I grin wickedly at him.

"I know this is an imposition," Allan says, "but I can't tell you how much we appreciate this." He clears his throat. "Is this a good time to start, or—"

Jalen turns me around, wraps his arms around me, and gives me a passionate, open-mouthed kiss. It's the kind of kiss we don't do in front of other people, and the sensations go straight between my legs. His left hand goes down to my ass, grabbing my buttcheek over my short, flouncy skirt, but then he dips his hand below my skirt, to my thigh. He runs his hand up the back of my leg, under my skirt, and then there's nothing between my ass and his hand.

"Fuck," I whisper, "you're getting me wet."

"You're already wet," he says. "Talking about fucking me in front of Alicia really turned you on."

I reach down and undo the top button on his jeans. His cock is rock-hard. "You ready to see this, Alicia?" I ask, just loud enough for her to hear. "You want to see what I get to take in my pussy every night when you aren't sending him to Switzerland?" I unzip his fly with one hand and reach into his underwear with the other, and with a deft touch, his cock is out, rigid and pulsing in my hand ever so slightly. The vein that runs down the bottom of his shaft is prominent. I hold it up for Alicia to see in all its glory before I run my nails lightly from his balls up his shaft, just below his corona.

"You never did that to his cock in high school, did you, Alicia? You wanted everyone to believe you were the hottest thing in Phoenix, but you can't hold a candle to me. Jalen doesn't want you, Alicia. He never did. He'd see me coming down the hall, all ass and tits and jiggly bits, and he'd get harder watching me with all my clothes on than he did with you when your clothes were *off*." I have no idea if this is true. Curious as I was, I never wanted to know how far Jalen and Alicia had gone, and when we started sleeping together in college, she wasn't even around anymore. I knew I couldn't ask anything about her without seeming obsessed or crazy, and honestly, after a few months, it didn't occur to me.

But Alicia is both obsessed *and* crazy, and she's writhing in her tight dress, her nipples hard and obscenely visible, as her eyes widen more and more, and her breathing gets sharper with each intake of breath.

"Maybe I'll lick his big dick now," I say, and Alicia moans. "You'd like to lick it, wouldn't you, Alicia? You'd *love* to take his beautiful, huge cock in your mouth."

"Please," Alicia says, and that gets her another yank on the leash. But this time, Alicia's having none of it. "Yes, Rachel, yes, put it in your mouth, please, I—"

Allan gives the leash a harder yank and steps in front of her so she can't see. She gives a strained cry, like she's a two-year-old who just dropped her ice cream. "Don't interrupt them," he says, gritting his teeth. "That was part of the deal."

For a fleeting moment, I wonder who's watching their kids, but then I remember that his family lives in the area. I wonder what Allan told them they'd be doing tonight when he dropped the kids off. Probably not bondage and voyeurism.

I continue, especially now that Alicia can't see me. I lick his shaft all the way up, being as loud as possible, and make noises like it's the most delicious thing I've ever tasted. Which it kind of is. "I mean, how can you put this monster in your mouth and *not* get married to the man attached to it?" I ask, moaning a little. "Oh, look—precum!" I act like it's the most precious artifact in the universe and I'm particularly noisy, siphoning it off the tip of his cock.

Alicia lets out a loud, guttural groan.

"Oh, baby girl," I say, "it's too bad you don't get to play with us." I stand back up. "What do you think, Jalen?"

"I think I'm going to fuck you senseless," he growls, and then he picks me up off the ground, over his shoulder in a fireman's carry. *Holy shit.* The pleasure floods everywhere in my body. He's never done this to me before; he's never been so alpha-male, like I have no say in the matter.

He walks over the sofa where we made love not an hour before and drops me there, being fairly gentle, but making it look as rough as possible for our audience. I squeal, louder than I needed to. My left leg is up on the back of the sofa, and my right foot is on the ground, so my legs are spread apart, my skirt around my waist, giving Alicia a full view.

"Oh my God," Alicia says, her eyes wide open.

Allan pulls Alicia close to him and whispers in her ear, and then he reaches down. Although I can't see where his hand goes, the hem of her dress moves. Her eyes lose focus for a moment. Then she takes a long, slow, languid breath, and looks at me as if to ask what I'm waiting for.

"Let's give her a good show," Jalen says, pushing his jeans completely down. I watch his hard cock bounce up and down as he kicks his feet out of his pants. He steps in front of me on the sofa, facing away from Alicia, who has started to buck her hips.

"He's got an amazing ass, doesn't he, Alicia?" I moan. "It's even better than it was when the two of you were dating."

She flinches slightly at my words, but Allan whispers into her ear again, and she nods and squeaks out a response. "Yes, he's got an amazing ass."

Jalen kneels on the sofa between my wide-spread legs, his erection about a foot from me. "Can you see all of this, Alicia?" he asks. "Is this what you wanted?"

"Yes," Alicia moans.

I bring my hands to my chest, and start lightly kneading

my left breast with one hand and at the same time tease my right nipple with the fingers of my other hand. "You wish you had big, sexy tits like mine, too, don't you, Alicia? The kind of tits that Jalen can't keep his eyes off."

"Or my hands," Jalen says, putting his left hand over my right breast, giving me a gentle squeeze.

"Play with my nipple like I was doing," I whisper. "That felt really good."

He complies, moving his hand so that his whole hand is still on my boob but my nipple pops out between his first two fingers. He pulls my nipple up a little, giving it a little tug, and I close my eyes and exhale. "Mmm," I say, "I like that, Jalen."

"I love being with you," Jalen says softly, low enough that the others can't hear. "I love how clever you were to catch Alicia doing this, and I love how smart you are."

"And I love how you want to take care of me and make sure that everything's okay."

"I would have quit my job for you, Rachel. You mean the world to me."

He bends down over me, holding himself steady with his free arm on the back of the sofa, and he kisses me on the lips, soft and gentle, once, then twice. I look in his face just as he opens his eyes after the kiss, and then I raise up just slightly, parting my lips, and we're kissing again, fully, deeply. His hard, eager cock pushes at my entrance—and then slips right in.

I break from the kiss. "Oh," I moan. "Fuck, Jalen."

He exhales. "God, you feel so good, Rachel. I love your body underneath me."

I move my left hand from my breast around to his back,

lightly running my hands from his shoulder blade down to his perfect ass, and I give his right cheek a firm, gentle squeeze. I want him to start his motion, I want him pumping his cock in and out of me, and I want Alicia to feel the pain of her first boyfriend fucking me instead of her. All the anger and hurt she's caused me the last few days, keeping him away from me, is erased in this moment.

"Not yet, my girl." He leans his head down on the sofa pillow that's halfway under my head. "Yesterday, I was yours," he said, "but today, you'll be mine."

"Oh yes," I say, and then I bite my lip. "You're going to do anything you want to me, aren't you?"

"That's right, baby. Anything I want."

I put my right hand on his hip and try to pull him toward me.

"Not yet, I said." Jalen takes his left hand off my boob, grabs my wrist and moves my hand from his hip to above my head. I take my left hand off his ass and move it above my head too, crossing my wrists, so that I have both hands over my head. Jalen slides his large hand, the one that can palm a basketball and dominate other teams, to cover the place where my wrists cross each over.

"Yes, Jalen," I whisper. "I'm yours."

"Oh my God," Alicia says in a high-pitched simper from across the room. "Oh God, Jalen, she's your dirty little whore. Make her—"

"Enough," Allan says, quietly but firmly, and I hear a smack and then Alicia's sharp intake of breath.

"Alicia really wants to be your dirty little whore," I moan, loud enough for our guests to hear, "but she's not. *I* am. I'm your dirty little whore. I'll do anything you want, Jalen. Anything."

And that does it. He thrusts in my deliciously wet pussy and then slides out. I can feel the restraint in his muscles—he wants to do this slow, make it last a long time—but he's so turned on by me and my complete domination of his ex that he's going faster than he wants to.

"She's not going anywhere," I say. "She's stuck on that side of the room, just watching your huge cock slide in and out of me. Wishing it was her underneath you, hands above her head, doing anything you want."

"You're the most beautiful woman in the world, Rachel," he says, his breaths coming sharper and faster.

I look over at Alicia, and her face is pinched tight. It's like she doesn't understand how Jalen can think I'm more beautiful than she is. *Well, you have to accept it, bitch, because it's true.*

Jalen's hips buck harder as his thrusts gain speed and urgency. I want to move my hands to roam all over his taut muscles, his fantastic body, but I push against his hand and he tightens his grip around my wrists. I start pushing against his pelvis, changing up the angle. I'm rewarded with some indirect stimulation on my clit. I moan, long and low. If Jalen keeps this up, it'll be a slow, wonderful session, and having an audience is just ramping up all the sensations.

I close my eyes but I can still hear the low squeals of my nemesis as her husband is doing *something* to her, his hand not visible underneath her tight, slutty dress. I bet Jalen would love to see *me* in a dress like that. He'd make last night's reading-and-screwing session look like a rehearsal.

He shifts his position just slightly, and the angle of the

stimulation is so much better. I have to bite my lip to keep from crying out, and Jalen kisses my neck, tracing his mouth down with licks and nibbles to my collarbone.

Alicia says something else, but I can't hear it with my eyes shut tight, concentrating on how good Jalen feels inside me. Then I hear the low rumble of Allan's voice, followed by a loud smack. I flinch, fighting to keep my eyes shut, and the pleasure turns up inside me.

"Oh, Jalen," I moan, my hips moving in time with his, "I'm about to come. Make me come with your huge cock."

Alicia groans and I decide to ramp up the dirty talk. "Fuck me, Jalen, fuck me with your big dick. Come inside me, baby. Let me feel everything."

"You're mine," Jalen says, kissing his way back up to my neck just below my ear. "Alicia wants me to own her the way I own you, but I only want you, Rachel."

"Oh—oh, Jalen, I'm so close."

"Don't come until I tell you to, Rachel."

"So close, Jalen—so close—"

"*Don't* come yet."

"Oh—Jalen—I don't know how much longer I can take it...."

"Not yet."

I speed my hips up and the friction from him gets right on top of my clit. "I can't hold it—"

"*Come.*"

And I do.

My orgasm hits me hard, and my arms go limp. All I feel is the electric rush between my legs and Jalen's hand, strong and forceful and loving, on my wrists. And then I feel his cock twitch and throb, and then he's gushing inside me too, as his low, guttural moans echo softly in my ears.

Slowly I come back to the real world and open my eyes. Alicia is coming too, quietly hitching her breath, eyes squeezed tight, her knees tight together. I free my left hand as Jalen's grip loosens after he comes, and I reach around his back, tracing my hand down to his ass.

"I love you, Jalen," I whisper in his ear.

"You can write something really hot about this later, right?"

I giggle. "I've already got my climactic scene."

Allan clears his throat. "I appreciate the two of you taking the time for Alicia today," he says, as though he just gave us a presentation on a timeshare in Palm Springs. "A million thanks. We'll get out of your hair, and I hope you have a great rest of your day."

Jalen rolls a little to the side so I can see Alicia.

Her blonde tresses are a mess, her upper chest is beet-red with a sex flush, and she's sucking on Allan's fingers. He pulls them out of her mouth. "What do you say?" he whispers to her, like he's talking to a misbehaving four-year-old.

"Thank you for letting me watch you fuck," Alicia says obediently.

"Good girl," he says, and I wonder what kind of sex life they have.

"You're beautiful, Rachel," Alicia says, unprompted. "I'm sorry I didn't see it before."

I'm shocked, but I murmur, "Thank you." I don't forgive her for what she's done. I'm not even sure she believes what she says. But I do appreciate that she made at least a small effort—and, of course, that she was the catalyst for the insane, humongous orgasm I just had.

Allan, still holding the leash, opens our front door and walks out with Alicia following him, tottering in her ridiculous heels. Jalen and I watch them go, and the door closes softly behind them.

THE NEXT STEPS

*S*till on top of me, Jalen clears his throat. "Did we just screw in front of my boss and her husband?"

I giggle. "She's your *former* boss, but yes, we did."

"I wasn't dreaming it?"

"Nope."

"Was she actually on a leash?"

"She sure was." I wiggle a little under him.

"Does that—does that make you hot?"

I blush. "Maybe a little. I bet you'd like to see me in a tight dress like that, and slutty heels too."

Jalen smiles wickedly. "Maybe. But the leash too?"

"I don't know. We could try, um, some things. I liked you holding my wrists above my head. Maybe I'd like the leash." Then I remember some of the fantasies I had when Jalen was traveling so much, and it makes me blush.

"What is it? There's more?"

"Umm... a couple of months ago, when you were in Zurich, I looked into a sex swing."

"You mean, like, *buying* one?"

I smile, a little nervously. "Yeah. I had it in my online shopping cart and everything. It sort of requires a lot of work to put together, though. I was hoping to surprise you when you came home from a trip, but the instructions talked about finding ceiling beams for the right weight distribution, and I wasn't sure if I'd have to get it professionally installed. The whole thing was a little overwhelming."

"A sex swing?"

"Yes."

Jalen studies my face for a minute. "But you still want one?"

I shift a little uncomfortably underneath him. "Maybe. I mean, a leather collar and a leash would be cheaper and less damaging to our walls."

A grin spreads over his face. "Man, I *hate* that I was in Zurich for two weeks a month." He pauses. "I'm going to get up now. You might want to change your position so we don't have to do anything dramatic to clean the upholstery on the couch."

"What do you mean, *we*?" I giggle. "You're the one who made the mess. She's *your* ex. And it's *your* jizz."

"Fine—just, you know, try not to get anything anywhere until I get back with a few towels." He pulls out of me with a loud slurping noise. He literally runs to the linen closet and is back with three of our old towels less than fifteen seconds later.

We start to clean up in thoughtful silence.

Jalen says, "I hope this doesn't complicate things at work. Once I saw how into it you were, I kind of threw caution to the wind."

"I'm pretty sure you'll be fine." I finish wiping up and

hand him the towel. "*We'll* be fine. It kind of feels like a weight's been lifted off my shoulders. Especially after all the shit she pulled since she became your boss."

"Sure doesn't feel like that was only a few days ago when it felt like she had us wrapped around her finger." He gathers all the towels and walks out of the room.

I stand up, the skirt still around my waist, and pull it down. I retrace my steps from our sex session earlier and pick up my bra and panties from the floor. I walk back through the house, still feeling a little naughty, my boobs jiggling and without underwear on. Jalen is in the laundry room, still naked, putting the towels we just used in the washing machine along with a few dish towels and a throw blanket. "You have anything else to go in?"

I nod as I look at his beautiful body, up and down. "Did you get the bath towels?"

"Already in there." He puts in a capful of liquid detergent, closes the door, and starts the wash cycle.

I wrap my arms around him from behind, my hands on his chest and stomach, and I press my body against his back, resting my head just above his shoulder blade. "I love you, Jalen."

"I love you, too."

"And I don't need a sex swing or screwing in front of strangers to know that I'm glad I married you and I'm happy to be spending my life with you."

"I'm so glad I'm home," he says softly. "I promise never to travel this much again, okay?"

"That's fine with me."

Jalen turns in my embrace until he's facing me, and then he takes my face in his hands and kisses me deeply. It's not the urgent, feral passion it was when he fucked me in front of Alicia. It's gentle. I feel safe and warm and loved.

"This is where I want to be."

"Me too."

"And," Jalen says, "I bet you'll be able to write a hell of a sequel to that werewolf story."

I hold him tighter. "I've got everything I need to inspire me right here."

Sign up for Marcus and Misty Oakwood's newsletter:
www.marcusandmisty.com

We hope you enjoyed reading this book as much as we enjoyed writing it. If you did, we'd sincerely appreciate a review on your favorite book retailer's website, Goodreads, and BookBub. Reviews are crucial for the success of books, and even just a line or two makes a huge difference.

—*Marcus and Misty*

www.ingramcontent.com/pod-product-compliance
Lightning Source LLC
Chambersburg PA
CBHW031944240626
47153CB00003B/858